D1482428

HER OLD-FASHIONED HUSBAND

LAYLAH ROBERTS

Laylah Roberts

Her Old-Fashioned Husband

© 2012, Laylah Roberts

Re-published ©2018, Laylah Roberts

Laylah.roberts@gmail.com

ALL RIGHTS RESERVED. This book contains material protected under
International and Federal Copyright Laws and Treaties. Any unauthorized reprint or
use of this material is prohibited. No part of this book may be reproduced or
transmitted in any form or by any means, electronic or mechanical, including
photocopying, recording, or by any information storage and retrieval system without
express written permission from the author / publisher.

Cover Design by: Spellbound Designs

❁ Created with Vellum

LET'S KEEP IN TOUCH!

Don't miss a new release, sign up to my newsletter for sneak peeks, deleted scenes and giveaways: https://landing.mailerlite.com/web-forms/landing/p7l6go

You can also join my Facebook readers group here: https://www.facebook.com/groups/386830425069911/

.

BOOKS BY LAYLAH ROBERTS

Doms of Decadence

Just for You, Sir

Forever Yours, Sir

For the Love of Sir

Sinfully Yours, Sir

Make me, Sir

A Taste of Sir

To Save Sir

Sir's Redemption

Reveal Me, Sir

Montana Daddies

Daddy Bear

Daddy's Little Darling

Daddy's Naughty Darling Novella

Daddy's Sweet Girl

Daddy's Lost Love

A Montana Daddies Christmas

Daring Daddy

Warrior Daddy

Daddy's Angel

Heal Me, Daddy

Daddy in Cowboy Boots

A Little Christmas Cheer

PROLOGUE

T *welve years ago...*

STU PRESSED her against the wall and shoved his hand beneath her t-shirt, his movements clumsy and rough. He worked his way up to her breast as Frankie tried to hide a shudder of revulsion.

She wanted to shove him away. Instead, she forced herself remain still. It was important that she keep him happy, and pushing him away was definitely going to piss him off.

Stu was popular. He had a car. He had a fake ID. He knew where all the parties were.

And perhaps, most importantly of all, because he lived in the next town, he didn't know her brothers. If he did, he'd be too scared to ever help her sneak off to parties and get drunk.

While she was grateful for his help, she wasn't going to sleep with him, though. But she had decided to throw him a bone— which was why she was suffering through his hand currently squeezing her breast to the point of bruising as his hot, sweet breath bathed her face. He leaned in for a kiss and Frankie quickly closed her eyes.

Stu slipped his tongue inside her mouth, making her shudder in revulsion. Ick, his breath stunk. She barely managed not to gag.

At nineteen, Stu might be four years older than her, but he was still gangly and immature. He had pimples for God's sake. No, she wasn't interested in him at all. Now, if it was Tom Sanders kissing her, Frankie would be melting at the knees. She bet Tom didn't slobber like a bulldog when he kissed a girl.

Tom was her brother, Brax's friend, and truly the most gorgeous boy Frankie had ever met. He was the same age as slobbery Stu, but worlds apart in immaturity and looks. With his dark hair, deep brown eyes and sexy grin, Tom could have graced any magazine cover. Stu was just lucky she didn't punch him in the nose.

Frankie turned her head and pushed her hands against his chest.

"No, Stu," she told him.

He stared at her through eyes glazed from too much alcohol and pot. What a loser.

Yeah, well, what does that make me, then?

Coming here tonight was a stupid idea. But she didn't care. *She didn't.* What else did she have to do? Sit in her room and think about her parents? She blinked back tears. No crying. She hadn't cried since her mom and dad died in a car crash three months ago. She wasn't about to start bawling now. If she did, then she didn't know if she'd ever stop.

"Come'n, Frankie," Stu slurred. "Don't be a bitch."

"How am I being a bitch by asking you not to paw me?" she snapped, irritated. She was starting to think that this wasn't worth the hassle.

Frankie pulled at his arm, trying to tug it away from under her shirt.

"You owe me." He glared down at her, his eyes darkening with anger.

Crap.

"How do you figure that?" she asked belligerently. He crowded closer. Frankie didn't have anywhere to go. She was already pressed up against the living room wall. She didn't even know exactly where she was. Stu had picked her up at their meeting place and driven her to this party, which wasn't even much of a party.

Fuck.

Alarm bells rang in her head. For a skinny guy, he was looking awfully large all of a sudden.

"Back off, Stu, I don't owe you a fucking thing."

She held back a wince as she swore, half-expecting someone to scold her. Swearing in her house would get her a good scolding for sure.

Not that anyone had told her off lately. She'd let a four-letter word slip yesterday in front of Kent, her second oldest brother, and he hadn't even blinked.

Frankie supposed without her parents here to enforce the rules; her brothers didn't care much what she did.

So why did you sneak out to of the house instead of telling Heath where you were going?

Her oldest brother was also the most serious. He wasn't one to bend or compromise. A rule was a rule. And Frankie had broken so many. Her curfew. Leaving the house without telling anyone where she was going. Hanging out with people her family hadn't met. Drinking. Smoking.

Yep, if Heath ever caught her, she was dead meat. Her ass would ache for days. Or else he'd ignore her, like all her brothers seemed to be doing lately. She wasn't really sure what was worse. Being forgotten or suffering through a spanking.

Stu crowded even closer, pushing his leg between hers. Panic clawed at her as she attempted to push him back. Damn it, he was stronger than he looked.

"You owe me this. You've been leading me on. Who's been picking you up, driving you around? Who bought you that beer? Hmm? What do you think you have between your legs, fucking gold?"

"Fuck you." She pushed at him, pounding her fists uselessly against his chest. "Get off me!" Surely that would bring one of their group to her rescue.

"Hey, Stu, you need some help there?" One of the boys yelled. The others snickered.

Stu's face went bright red.

Shit. Not good.

Frankie struggled in earnest, using her legs, her hands, her teeth, everything she could to get away from the asshole pawing at her.

Her t-shirt ripped as he clawed at it. His hand on her breast was bruising. Her heart pounded so fast she thought she might faint. But she couldn't faint. Then he would win.

Tiring, she'd started sobbing when suddenly he was gone and before her was a broad back covered in a blue t-shirt. Frankie gasped frantically, her entire body shaking with fear and shock.

"Get up, asshole, so I can push you back down," the guy standing between her and Stu demanded.

Frankie swayed. She swore that was Tom speaking. But couldn't be possible. What would Tom be doing here?

"T-Tom?" she asked quietly, hating the way her voice shook.

Tom turned to look at her and the fury on his face took her breath away. His face softened slightly as he studied her face.

Then he dropped his gaze to her ripped t-shirt and his eyes grew dark, stormy. Furious.

She hastily pulled the pieces of her shirt together, crossing her arms over her chest. He turned around again, his body stiff with tension. Frankie peered around his back to see Stu pick himself up off the ground.

"What the hell do you think you're doing? She's my girlfriend, we were just having fun," Stu whined. God, he was a dick.

"That true, Frankie?" Tom asked without looking back at her. "Were you having fun?"

"No," she spat out in disgust. She tried to move around Tom to face Stu, but Tom swung his arm back, holding her behind him.

"Stay put," he ordered. Frankie stilled in surprise. He'd never spoken to her like that before. Tears welled in her eyes. She blinked them back. She was tougher than this.

Tom pointed at Stu. "Touch her again, hell, even look at her again and I will make sure you sing soprano for the rest of your life. Got me?"

"Ooh, I'm so scared," Stu said with false bravado. "What you gonna do about it?"

Tom swung his arm back and punched Stu in the nose. Frankie winced as Stu squealed.

"That's what I'm gonna do," he told Stu calmly.

Frankie ducked around to one side, ignoring Tom's growl of warning.

Stu stared up at his friends as he lay on the ground, his nose dripping blood. Tom had obviously broken it. He wasn't the type to go around swinging punches. He was always so calm. She swallowed heavily. What would happen now? Would Stu's dickhead friends retaliate?

"Why are you guys just standing around?" Stu whined

"If he wants to take the bitch, let him, Stu," Vince sneered, looking her over. Asshole. She'd never liked him. "She's not worth fighting over."

Stu's face grew splotchy from a mix of embarrassment and anger. Not attractive. "What the fuck you saying, Vince? You're not going to back me against this asshole? He's one guy, we can easily take him."

"Yeah, but I've seen him playing ball," Vince replied, eyeing Tom nervously. "He's tough, man. Just leave it alone."

A couple of the others nodded.

The few girls in the group stared at Tom with a combination of admiration and lust. Frankie glared at them.

"Never touch her again," Tom growled.

Frankie felt a surge of satisfaction at his protectiveness. When her brothers got this way, it was annoying. With Tom, well, it made her stomach dance.

"Frankie, let's go."

Tom turned and held out his hand. Frankie took it, using her other hand to hold her t-shirt together. She rushed to keep up with Tom who set a brisk pace through the house.

"Wait, slow down." Digging her heels in, Frankie tried desperately to get him to stop.

She'd known Tom for years—he'd spent half his childhood at their house. Now that he attended college she saw less of him, which was a damn shame.

Because she still had one hell of a crush on him.

Right now, though, she was confused as hell about what he was doing here. And why he was in such a rush.

"Tom, let me go," she'd demanded, tugging at the arm he held as he continued to half-drag her through the house. "Can't you slow down?" They stepped outside. The long driveway held several cars.

"No," Tom snapped. "Now move before they decide they want a fight and come after us."

When she made no move to speed up, Tom turned and crouching, slung her over his shoulder.

"Tom!"

He walked steadily down the drive, ignoring her.

"Put me down." Kicking, squirming, she tried desperately to free herself. This was so embarrassing. What if someone she knew saw her? Sure, she might get points for being with Tom, who had been really popular at school, but being held in this position was humiliating. Instead of putting her down, he simply placed his arm over her thighs to keep her legs still.

"Settle down now, Frankie," he ordered in a low voice. "I know you've had a fright but that's no excuse for acting like a brat."

She pounded her hands down on his back. *How dare he! A brat?*

A heavy whack landed on her ass. She gasped.

"Tom, what the fuck?"

He growled. "You are just asking for a spanking, little one. Calm yourself, before I do it for you."

"How?" she screeched. "By spanking me?"

"Yes," he said calmly.

Shit, she'd fallen for a guy just like her brothers. Oh, no way. Her brothers believed in spanking as a method of correcting behavior—all of them had roasted her ass for one thing or another in her life. Didn't help that she was the youngest, and a complete brat according to her brother, Cam.

But there was no way was she accepting a spanking from anyone else. Hell, she was too old to be spanked anyway. She'd be sixteen soon.

"Put me down," she demanded coolly.

"No, I need to get you home and with the way you were dawdling, this is the quickest way to do it."

"I am not going home with you, you jerk."

Smack! Damn this was humiliating. The guy she'd idolized for years, daydreamed about marrying, even practiced her signature using his last name, was treating her like a two-year-old throwing a tantrum!

"Language. And you certainly are coming home with me. No way am I leaving you here to get raped by that asshole."

He stopped and pulled her right side up. She swayed, the sudden movement combined with the alcohol she'd drunk making her less than steady. "You're exaggerating. Stu wouldn't have raped me."

"It sure looked like things were headed that way to me," Tom said darkly. "And you weren't exactly getting anywhere trying to fight him off. A little bit like you had no chance."

He held her steady, his hand sure and steady on her hip.

Frankie couldn't help but compare him to Stu. Where Stu immature and boyish, Tom seemed old beyond his twenty years.

"I'm not little," she muttered. At nearly five-foot-eight, she'd always been taller than the other girls in her class.

He tapped her nose. "You are to me."

She leaned in closer, drawn to the scent of him, his warmth, his strength.

"Tom?" she murmured.

"Yes?" he asked.

"Kiss me?"

His gaze widened and for a moment she thought he was going to do it. Then he shook his head and stood back, opening the door to his truck.

"Get in," he demanded.

Crushed, horribly embarrassed, she turned away. "Fuck you."

She managed to take a step before he grabbed her arm, hauling her back.

"Little girl, you are in serious need of a spanking."

For a moment, she thought he was going to do it. Her breath caught in her throat. Then he shook his head. "But now isn't the time, you've just had a fright."

"Let me go."

"I can't do that, honey." He clasped her cheeks in his hands. "Frankie, I am not kissing you while you're drunk, minutes after you were mauled." He grimaced. "Don't you have any self-preservation, girl?"

Hope unfurled. Did that mean he wanted to kiss her?

"I'm not drunk," she denied.

Shaking his head, Tom clasped her around the waist and lifted her into the passenger seat of his truck. Leaning across, he did up her belt.

"I'm not a kid," she complained, but he ignored her, shutting the door before making his way around to the driver's side. Frankie folded her arms across her chest, staring mulishly out the window. Her stomach rolled slightly as they took off and she took a deep breath.

Tom glanced at her sharply. "Tell me if you're going to be sick."

She remained silent.

"Not speaking to me now?" he asked, his voice holding a hint of humor.

Frankie bit the inside of her mouth.

"What were you doing there, Frankie? How did you even get there? I take it you snuck out of the house. Did you catch a ride with one of those guys?"

His voice was incredulous, begging her to tell him she wasn't that stupid.

Frankie stared out the side window, not looking at him. Her emotions were all over the place. The shock of Stu attacking her, her mortification over Tom rejecting her, it was all a bit much. And it was all catching up on her at once. She sat on her hands to hide their shaking.

"Frankie, talk to me. This rebellious teenager stuff isn't you. What on earth were you thinking? How do you think your brothers would feel should anything happen to you? Do you even know any of those people? What if I hadn't turned up? What then? I know you have a brain, use it."

Suppressing her guilt, Frankie turned to him with what she hoped was a look of disdain.

"Well, if you think those guys are losers then what were you doing there? Why aren't you at college?"

"It's the holidays. I was driving a friend there and stopped in for a drink."

As they neared the driveway to her house, Frankie put her hand on the latch of her seatbelt, prepared to jump out and walk up the long drive so she could sneak back up the tree to get into her room.

Instead of stopping, Tom turned up the drive.

"What are you doing?" she gasped.

He didn't answer.

"Umm, Tom, there's no need to come up to the house. I'll walk," she said nervously.

"Honey, if you think I'm not escorting you inside and making sure you're in the care of one of your brothers, you're sadly mistaken."

She gaped at him in horror. "Heath will kill me."

Tom stared at her calmly. "He won't kill you, but he will ensure this doesn't happen again. Probably by spanking your ass scarlet."

"You cannot talk to me like that!" she squeaked.

He turned to her with a smile and her heart raced. He was so cute. Even when he was being an asshole.

"You're forgetting I've seen that butt of yours being spanked a time or two. You've always been a brat, Frankie. But you've never gone this far. You could have been really hurt. I'm worried about you. You can talk to me, you know."

Tom stared at her in concern as he stopped the truck.

Frankie shrugged, wishing she could confess her loneliness, her confusion, her need to find some respite from the grief of losing her parents. But instead she bit her lip, holding in her emotions.

She didn't wait for him to come around and open her door. Jumping out, she ran up to the porch, trying to get inside and up to her bedroom before Tom reached the house. But he suddenly appeared beside her and grabbing her hand, tugged her towards Heath's study.

Stopping outside, he knocked on the closed door.

"Come in," Heath called out. Frankie winced at the tiredness in her oldest brother's voice. Tugging her in, Tom closed the door behind them with an ominous thud.

By this time, Frankie's heart was going a mile a minute, her palms sweating, her stomach rolling nauseously. This was not happening.

Heath stared at them in surprise, his face tired and lined. Guilt filled her. Heath didn't need this on top of everything else he had to worry about. He'd not only become her guardian but he had a huge ranch to run. Even with Kent and Cam's help it was still a lot for him to take on.

Maybe she should leave home. She was old enough to get a job. She was just a burden and a trouble maker.

"What's going on? Tom, what are you doing here?"

Heath's gaze narrowed in on Frankie. Heath was so like her Daddy, sometimes it hurt her to look at him. Tears filled her eyes as she glanced away.

"Frankie, sweetheart? What's wrong?" Heath asked, his voice filled with concern. "How did your t-shirt get ripped?" His voice grew darker, more demanding.

With a sob, she shook her head.

"Tell him, Frankie," Tom urged her.

"I can't," she wailed.

"Frankie, look at me." She raised her gaze to meet her brother's. He pushed his chair back from the desk and held his arms open, waiting. Frankie flew at him and he gathered her on her lap, rocking her gently.

"What's wrong, little girl, hmm?" he asked. "What's happened? Has someone hurt you?"

She could feel his alarm as she gulped for breath.

"Frankie," Heath said firmly. "You're scaring me, sweetheart. Calm down and tell me what's going on."

Slowly, she settled to the point she could talk. "I'm so sorry, Heath. I-I really am."

"Tell me. We can figure it out together." Those few words broke the dam and she told him everything.

"I snuck out of the house and this guy, Stu, picked me up at the bottom of the drive. I knew you were busy and the others are out on dates and stuff. Stu took me to this party over in Bronwood. I didn't really know anyone there."

"Who is this Stu?" Heath asked, running his hand up and down her back. She didn't deserve his comfort.

Frankie shrugged. "Just this guy I met one time at Amy's. He's a friend of her older brother's. He asked me out to a party about a month ago."

Heath remained calm. "Did they have alcohol at this party?"

"Yes. I only had three beers," she said in a rush.

"Hmm." He kissed her forehead and she collapsed against him, relieved he wasn't furious. She knew Heath loved her, but since her parents died she'd had this fear that he would grow sick of her. He was only twenty-seven—he had a life of his own to live without looking after a teenage brat.

"And you were at this party, Tom?" Heath asked.

She stiffened. She'd hoped to keep some parts of what happened from Heath. If only Tom would leave then she could keep the rest a secret. Why hadn't he left? Hadn't he caused her enough problems already?

"I went there with a friend," Tom began. "I went inside for a drink. When I saw her, this guy, Stu, was practically mauling her. She was trying to fight him off, but he's a lot bigger than she is, and she was easily overpowered."

"I would have gotten him off me eventually," Frankie muttered. "It's not like that's the first time he's tried it on."

She sucked in a breath, wishing she could take those words back.

Both men stilled and stared at her.

"What?" Heath asked, his voice a quiet whisper.

Uh oh.

Frankie squirmed.

"Frankie," Tom said in a cold voice. "What do you mean this isn't the first time? He's attacked you before?"

"He wasn't really attacking me. We were making out." Although this time he'd been much more persistent. Normally she could just push him off. Surely he wouldn't have taken it much further. She could have fought him off. Right?

Frankie felt sick. What if she hadn't been able to? What if he'd kept going? Tom really had saved her.

She dropped her gaze to her hands.

"Frankie, how many times have you snuck out with this guy?" Heath asked.

She clenched her hands into fists.

"A few," she admitted. "He always tries to kiss me and stuff. This time, though, he was pretty persistent. I was telling him no, trying to push him away when Tom pulled him off me. Stu went flying. Tom then pulled me out of the house."

She bit her lip to hold in a sob.

Heath started rocking her again, his hand running up and down her back. She buried her head against his chest.

"I should have killed the fucking bastard," Tom swore, surprising her.

"Don't worry about it," Heath told him. "Write down the address of this party and I'll take care of it all."

Frankie knew Stu was going to be sorry he was ever born, but she couldn't bring herself to feel any sympathy for him.

"I owe you a big debt, Tom," Heath said.

"None needed. I'm just glad you're all right. Frankie, I'll see you later, okay?"

Frankie remained silent, keeping her face hidden against Heath's chest.

"Frankie," Heath warned. "What do you say?"

"See you," she muttered ungraciously.

Heath sighed. "Frankie, you can do better than that." His voice was low. She bit her lip to stop herself from immediately obeying him.

"It's okay, I know I'm not her favorite person right now," Tom told Heath as though she weren't there.

"Yeah, well, I'm soon to top that list," Heath told him grimly.

Frankie said nothing, just sat there feeling a mixture of anger and relief.

When the door closed, she raised her head and looked up at her brother.

"That wasn't very well done of you, kid. He did you a favor by getting you out of there and bringing you safely home."

"He carried me over his shoulder and spanked my butt!" she protested.

"Sounds like you deserved it. Why are you so mad? He helped you, Frankie. Doesn't sound like anyone else tried to."

"It was humiliating," she admitted.

"Did he hurt you in any way?"

She shook her head. Those few smacks hadn't even registered. She'd sure had worse.

"You realize you're getting another punishment, don't you?" he said softly, his voice gentle as he continued to rub his hand over her back.

Yeah, she'd figured that. Tears welled in her eyes.

"I'm not a child, Heath."

"You're fifteen, sweetheart. You're a baby. You've got no business sneaking out of the house to go off with a guy. Then there's the drinking. How old is this Stu?"

"Nearly twenty."

"Still too young to buy alcohol, I'm guessing he's got a fake ID."

She nodded, chewing her lip. "Are you really angry at me, Heath?" He was the brother she adored most. Heath had the most patience of all her brothers, and he'd always had time to answer her questions or push her on the swing when she was little. Even once he'd left home, whenever he visited, they'd do something together, just the two of them.

Heath sighed. "When I was seventeen, my best friend's older brother got a fake ID."

"Really?"

He nodded. "He bought a stash of beer and hid it in the trunk of his car. My friend Mac and I found it one day. We stole a box then took off into the woods. Drunk ourselves silly. Mac's old man found us a few hours later and hauled us home."

"What happened then?" she asked in disbelief. Heath was so sensible, so mature; it was hard to ever believe he did this.

"He took me home. I was so drunk that Dad had to put me to bed. The next day, though, boy did I pay the piper."

"He punished you?" She didn't remember this at all. But then she'd only have been around six or seven at the time.

"Oh yeah. You and Mom were away in the city shopping. He hauled me up early in the morning, told me to shower and get into his study. I stood just where you were standing earlier, hung over, feeling really sorry for myself while he lectured me on responsibility, on looking after myself. Jeez, by the end of it I was ready to beg him to punish me so I could lie down and feel sorry for myself."

"How did he punish you?"

At seventeen, Heath would have been nearly as big as he was now. He'd filled out more, but he would have been taller than their father.

"He told me I was too big for a whipping, which I was relieved about, foolishly. Instead, after breakfast, he sent me to the barn to clean out all the stalls. I had to shovel shit with my head throbbing and my stomach heaving. I'd have gladly taken some licks of the belt by the end of the day. Damn, he worked me hard all weekend. I never touched alcohol again until I hit legal age."

"That was rough. Did you resent him for it?"

"No, baby. You know how punishment works in this house. Once you're punished all is forgiven."

"Are you going to make me muck out stalls tomorrow?" she asked.

He chuckled. "Probably should. But no." He ran his hand over her head. "But I do have to punish you, though, you know that right?"

She nodded.

"You're so much more vulnerable than I am. That bastard could have really hurt you. What were you thinking, baby? Don't you know how devastated we'd all be if something happened to you?"

She shrugged.

"Frankie," he warned.

"I-I just miss Mama and Daddy so much, Heath," she cried, burying her face against his chest. "I'm so sad all the time and lonely. I just wanted to do something to forget."

"Ahh, honey." He squeezed her tight. "I miss them, too. We all do. Why didn't you come to me and tell me you were struggling?"

"Because you're so busy with the ranch. I didn't want to bother you." She held back the threatening tears through sheer force of will, her breath coming in sharp, short pants.

"Frankie, I want you to calm down and look at me, because what I have to say is very important."

Frankie attempted to slow her racing heart as she stared up at him.

"Nothing is as important to me as you, Brax, Cam, and Kent. If I need to sell this place and devote my time to you guys then I will, got it?"

"But that's not fair to you!" she cried.

He shook his head, smiling faintly. "Ahh, honey. Don't you understand? All I want is you guys to be healthy, happy and safe. That is what makes me happy. It has nothing to do with fairness."

"I'm really sorry, Heath. I just felt so numb, you know. I guess-I guess maybe I wanted to be found out."

"I know, baby. I think it might be a good idea if we find someone for you to talk to about your loss."

Frankie gaped at him. "What? Like a shrink? I'm not crazy."

"I don't think you're crazy," he said patiently. "You're grieving. We all are. Perhaps we all need to see a grief counselor."

"You too?" she asked.

He nodded. "Me as well."

"Well, I guess if you go to one, I can too."

"Brave girl," he praised her. "How about you go hop into bed, I'll come up soon and tuck you in. You look exhausted."

She was. She hadn't been sleeping well. Her dreams were filled with her parents, only for her to wake up and realize that they were just dreams and her parents really were gone.

"Aren't you going to punish me?" she asked.

"I think that can wait until tomorrow, you've had a real fright tonight."

"I'd rather get it over and done with."

He watched her, then rubbed his chin. "You sure?"

Her chin wobbled a little but she nodded her head. She wouldn't sleep if she had to worry over what punishment she would get.

"All right. I'm going to give you a choice."

Umm, what?

"A spanking gets the punishment over quickly and then we can get down to forgiveness. But I know you're getting older. We weren't really spanked once we got past fifteen. So what would you rather? A spanking or to be grounded?"

Okay, this surprised her. And crazily, she found herself indecisive about what to choose.

"How long would I be grounded for?"

"How long you been sneaking out for?"

Crap. She knew she couldn't lie. "A month."

He nodded. "Sounds fair."

A whole month of being grounded. No phone. No T.V. No riding. She couldn't do it.

"I'll take the spanking," she whispered.

Heath nodded. "Think I would have chosen the same. All right, go put your nightie on and clean your teeth then come back down here."

Frankie stood and walked towards the door then moved up to her bedroom. She'd never gotten ready for bed so slowly. What had she been thinking, choosing a spanking?

Frankie took a deep breath as she stood outside Heath's study yet again. Then she knocked.

"Come in, honey."

"Come here, sweetheart," her brother ordered, his arms wide as he stood and moved towards her. She flew at him, making him chuckle as she held on tight. He kissed the top of her head.

"You know I love you, right?"

She nodded. "I love you, too."

"I never want you to be so lax with your safety again, Frankie, understand me?" He pulled back and looked down at her.

She nodded, swallowing heavily at the stern look in his eye.

"Good. Now, some rules. From now on, your bedtime is ten p.m. sharp."

Frankie opened her mouth in shock. She hadn't had a bedtime since she was a kid.

"But, Heath, Mom and Dad—"

"These are my rules for you, honey," he interrupted her gently. "I haven't wanted to bring this up because you've had enough change. However, I think you need more structure now than you had in the past. You've had a big upheaval in your life, you need to know your rules and boundaries, and that if you stray from them that there is someone who loves you enough to hold you accountable."

"That's so old school, Heath," she told him. But without any heat. She knew why he was doing it. Because he loved her.

"I know, baby. But it's what I believe. I'm an old-fashioned sort of guy. Let's get this over so you can get some sleep, okay?"

Yeah, like she'd be sleeping much after this.

But twenty minutes later, as she lay in bed with a throbbing ass, she felt herself drifting off to sleep. Although she hated to admit it, Tom had done her a favor by dragging her home. Not that she'd ever tell him that.

1

Frankie looked down at the clear strip on the pregnancy test, desperately willing it to give her the result she wanted. A red line appeared. Just one. She waited and waited. But there was only the one line.

Not pregnant.

She threw the tester across the bathroom, watching furiously as it banged against the wall then fell to the floor. Damn thing wouldn't even give her the satisfaction of shattering.

Like her insides were.

She slumped to the floor, her temper fading as sorrow overcame her. It had been a whole year. A year of no alcohol, of eating healthy, of hoping, and dreaming, and praying. A year's worth of failed tests and disappointment.

Tears ran down her cheeks.

What was wrong with her? She and Tom had been to see a fertility specialist. They'd done all the tests. Nothing had shown up. The specialist had told them both that it took longer for some people to get pregnant.

But how long was she expected to wait? She leaned her head

back against the bathroom wall. She was so tired. Tired of being a disappointment. Tired of trying and failing.

Tom may not show it, but she knew he was disappointed as well.

Frankie had watched him with her best friend, Anna's little boy. Tom looked at Jaron like he was the most precious thing in the world. It had to be a real letdown every time she told him they weren't pregnant.

But he didn't show his pain. He was such an Alpha male. No doubt he thought he had to stay strong for her. She'd started to get so depressed each month after all the negative results that Tom had told her that she wasn't to do any more tests without him.

But he was away at a conference in Seattle at the moment and she hadn't been about to wait two more days to take the test.

Frankie sighed and wiped her hands across her cheeks. Crying wasn't going to help a thing. Tiredly, she pulled herself up and, picking up the discarded tester, chucked it in the bin. Turning on the shower, she slowly undressed. Testing the water, she climbed into the cubicle, hoping the hot water would ease the tension in her muscles.

Maybe it just wasn't meant to be. She wasn't meant to be a mom. This was the universe's way of telling her she'd be crap. Probably true. She was sometimes selfish. She tended to be impulsive and she could be really blunt.

Yeah, maybe becoming a mother wasn't a good idea.

But Tom deserved to be a dad.

Tom was kind and patient. Loving. Smart. He was also breathtakingly handsome. He'd been cute as a teenager, but he'd grown more into his looks over the years. His dark brown hair went perfectly with his hazel-colored eyes and lightly tanned skin. Years of running had toned his long body, giving him a sleek, muscular appearance.

They'd had a rocky start. Tom was a few years older than

Frankie. He was good friends with her youngest brother, Brax. Growing up, he'd spent so much time at her house that he felt like a part of the family. As Frankie had grown older, she'd started noticing how cute he was. He'd never teased her the way her brothers did, instead he'd treated her like an adult.

She'd adored the ground he'd walked in.

Then her parents had died and Frankie had gone slightly off the rails. She'd gotten in with the wrong crowd. She'd started smoking, drinking. Amazingly, she'd been able to hide it from her brothers.

The night Tom had dragged her home from a party had changed things for her drastically. Heath started to pay much closer attention to her. Both a blessing and a curse. She loved having her brother's attention, and her behavior and school work had really improved.

Of course, she'd ended up getting spanked on a fairly regular basis until she'd settled down some. Heath had some very old-fashioned views and unfortunately, so did her husband.

After Tom dragged her out of that party, she'd hidden her feelings for him behind an angry mask, which had gotten her scolded plenty by her brothers. But she hadn't cared. She'd loved him. And he'd thought of her as a child.

Or so she'd believed.

A couple of years ago he'd moved back to Hammersly to open up his own practice. Frankie had been so nervous at the idea of seeing him again that she'd spent the few months before she was due to go home for Christmas nervously shopping and partying, spending money she didn't have. She'd acted horribly that Christmas, existing in a state of anxiety, swinging from anger to euphoria. Her mind had been so obsessed with Tom and seeing him, that she'd blocked everything else out.

Frankie had tried hard ever since to put others first. She loved her family, and was extremely protective of them. Like they were of her. She just wished she could have a family of her own.

What would Tom do if she couldn't get pregnant? What if there was something wrong with her and they could never have children? Would he leave her? Just the thought made her feel ill.

Feeling as though her heart were breaking into small pieces, Frankie finished up her shower, put on her fluffy pajamas, and traipsed down to the living room to watch television. She looked at the time. Eight. Tom would call any minute. She supposed she should eat, but she wasn't much in the mood. Her cell phone rang. She picked it up.

"Hi, honey," she said.

"Hello, baby," Tom said in that rich-as-honey voice of his.

Frankie immediately smiled, the knot in her stomach easing. "Hey, babe," she said warmly. "How are you? How's the conference going?"

She was so proud of Tom. He'd been asked to present a paper at this conference. He had a lot of job offers, but he was happy to stay here in his own practice. He and his partner, Jeff, had a busy practice, people came from miles around to them. Frankie wished she could have gone with him to this conference, but she couldn't get any time off work.

"The conference is going well. Presented my paper today, it seemed to be well received. You sound tired, Frankie."

"Just a bit," she admitted, knowing if she told him how truly exhausted she was he'd just worry.

"Hmm, why don't you call in sick tomorrow and rest?"

"I can't do that, Tom," she said shocked he'd even suggest it. "I'm not sick. I can't lie. You'd blister my butt if I ever suggested that."

Tom only really had a few rules for her. And they were ones she'd agreed to when she'd married him. Respect was the big one. And that meant no lying to each other. There were a few around safety, such as not texting while she was driving, which Frankie had been guilty of a few times.

Tom sighed. "I know, but I'm worried about you, sweetheart. When I left you looked pale and tired and now you sound exhausted. I wish you'd consider giving up your job."

"But I like nursing. Besides, what would I do all day?" This wasn't a new conversation. Tom often suggested she give up working.

"You could take up a hobby. I know you love photography."

"That wouldn't keep me busy. I wouldn't do well as a housewife."

Tom sighed. "I like the idea of taking care of you. I just want you to be happy and if you're honest with me and yourself, you know you're not happy at work."

Yeah, but she felt she needed to work. She needed to contribute to their household in some way.

"You don't need to be busy all day, Frankie," Tom replied patiently. "You need to rest as well, you're wearing yourself out. They work you too hard at your job. Wouldn't you like time to go riding? And to visit your brothers?" He dangled the suggestions out like they were Godiva chocolates—her favorite—and it was tempting.

Frankie hated having nothing to do, but lately it seemed like she was running on caffeine and nothing else. She was overtired, wired, and she needed a break. She knew they took advantage of her at work, getting her to do the job of two people simply because she was efficient and a hard worker.

"I'll think about it," she acquiesced.

"That's all I ask, baby. You know I just want what's best for you, don't you?"

Frankie snorted. "That's usually what you say before I get a spanking."

"Do you need a spanking?" he asked in a deep voice. Frankie shivered.

"Well, I have been a bit bad," she said. She didn't want a punishment spanking, of course, who would? But a fun spanking that led to amazing sex, now that she'd kill for right now.

"Hmm, I bet you have, I'll have to take care of that when I get home won't I? Turn you over my knee, bare that small bottom and take my hand to your white buttocks until they're glowing red. Is that what you need, Frankie, my darling?" he asked, his voice making her shiver with need. Her nipples hardened.

"Tom!" she squealed, surprised by this side of him. He'd never spoken to her so explicitly.

"Do you wish I was there, honey? Touching you? Squeezing your breasts, rubbing my thumbs over your nipples, do you wish I was doing that right now?"

"God, yes." She closed her eyes and ran a finger over her nipple, gasping at the feel of her own finger touching her hard nub.

"I can hear your breath quickening, Frankie. Are you being a bad girl and touching yourself?"

"Yes," she groaned as she pinched and pulled at her nipple. She lay back on the couch. "Please, Tom."

They'd never had phone sex before. But damn, he was making her hot. And she wanted more.

"Please what, Frankie?" he asked.

"Please tell me more, I want to come." She blushed as she said it, but there was no turning back now.

"Hmm, I'm not sure," he teased.

"Please, please," she cried. She couldn't stand it. Although he'd only been gone a few days, she was aching for him, her pussy throbbing, arousal scouring her body.

"All right, baby. Where is your hand right now?"

"On my breast," she replied with a groan.

"Are you playing with your nipple?" he crooned. "Are you pinching it? Is it hard, baby?"

"Yes, Tom," she replied, her insides melting.

He'd never taken charge in the bedroom like this before, but she couldn't deny how turned on it was making her. Tom was the head of their little household. And that was the way they both wanted it. He might not have a lot of rules, but they were strictly enforced.

Frankie knew she could always rely on Tom. He would always be there for her, no matter what. Sure, he could be bossy and obstinate and he often made her do things, 'for her own good', damned if she didn't hate that phrase. She just wished she could be everything he needed. Sometimes she felt like such a failure. And not just because she couldn't get pregnant. She often worried that she wasn't good enough for him. And that one day he'd realize that and leave her. She gulped.

"That's my good girl. Are you naked, baby?"

"No," she groaned.

"Get naked for me, honey."

Frankie pulled off her pajamas. The colder air hit her hot skin, making her shiver.

"Run your hand over your stomach, honey," Tom told her.

Frankie pressed her palm over her flat stomach.

"Move it down to your pussy, is it nice and smooth?"

"Yes, I just had it waxed."

"Good girl. I want you to cup yourself, honey. Don't touch your clit yet, though, just hold your palm over that sweet pussy."

Frankie whimpered. She was on fire, she had to come desperately.

"Please," she cried out.

"Listen to me, baby. I want you to stick me on speaker phone, okay? You're going to need both hands. Do it now."

With a groan, Frankie did as he ordered, then lay back on the couch.

"You're on speaker." Her voice was breathless. The need to come was already so strong.

"I bet your face is flushed with need, your chest rising and falling quickly with each breath. I want you to put one finger deep inside that sweet pussy. Are you wet, darling? Tell me how it feels."

"Hot, so hot," Frankie told him. "I'm so wet. I need to come so bad."

"I want you to lie on your back on the couch, curl your legs up to your chest and split them wide. Tell me when you're in position."

Her cheeks filling with heat, Frankie did as she was told, grateful no one could see her in this position, open, vulnerable. Not that Tom hadn't seen her like this before. Sometimes, he just liked to sit and stare at her, with all of her on full display. She both hated and loved that.

"I'm in position."

"Very good. I wish I could see you, darling. You know how much I like to look at that pretty pussy." The low croon of his voice soothed her at the same time as it excited her.

"Now put both hands on your breasts, I want you to cup them. Are you doing that, baby?"

"Yes," she replied in a breathless voice.

"Yes, Sir." His voice was dark. Deep. A warning. And she shivered in a mix of trepidation and excitement.

"What?"

"When I take control in the bedroom, you'll call me sir."

All right, this was new. But surprisingly, she kind of liked it. And she really liked having him take charge.

"Sorry, Sir."

"Very good, little girl."

She didn't know what it was about him taking charge that

turned her on so much, but she couldn't deny that it did. Her pussy was throbbing, her clit aching. Sometimes she'd worried there was something wrong with her because she needed his rules and guidance. But her brothers had similar relationships with their wives. Hell, poor Bryony had to contend with both Cam and Kent.

Frankie had her hands full with just one dominant man. Two and she'd never walk properly again. She giggled at the thought.

"Something funny, sweetheart?"

A lesser man might have been insulted or maybe self-conscious, but she heard a hint of lazy amusement in his voice.

"Just thinking that I'm glad I don't have two husbands or I'd never walk properly again."

"And you never will have another husband. No one touches you but me." The possession in his voice had her stomach rolling over in desire.

"Now, squeeze and pinch those hard, tight little nipples. Your breasts are beautiful, I could spend hours just nuzzling those breasts and licking those sweet nipples. How does that feel?"

"So good, Sir," she told him as she played with herself. Damn, listening to his dark commands was a huge turn on. She was close to exploding. "May I touch my clit?"

"Since you asked so nicely, yes you may. But listen closely to my orders and make sure you obey. You may not come until I tell you."

She whimpered softly, she hated holding back her orgasm.

"Pull your pussy lips apart with one hand. I want you to circle your clit. I bet that feels really good, doesn't it?"

"So good," she sighed. Better than good. Amazing. Wonderful. Stupendous. She was close, so close.

"Now press two fingers from your other hand inside that wet passage. Can you find that sweet spot inside you, baby?"

She pushed them deep. "I've found it, Sir."

"I want you to rub it with the tips of your fingers while you circle your clit. Are you doing as I say?"

Her breath sped up. Oh hell, it wouldn't take much to send her over. "Yes, it feels so good, so hot. I need to come so bad, I can feel it growing. Please," she begged. Her skin felt too tight, on fire, her body overflowing with heat.

"Not yet. Hold off. Be a good girl and wait until I say you can come."

"That's so mean," she complained. He was killing her.

Tom chuckled. "You'll thank me soon. Tap your clit now. How do you feel?"

"Like I'm going to explode."

"Are you hot?"

"Yes, God, yes."

"Flick your clit harder. I want you to pump your fingers in and out of your passage. Faster."

Her head thrashed as she followed his orders, his words driving her higher.

"I want to hear you come. I want to hear all those cries and whimpers. Come now, Francesca!"

She exploded, her body bucking off the couch as she screamed.

"Good girl, let it all out, come for me. Keep tapping that clit. Slowly," he crooned. "Come back to me now."

Still panting heavily, Frankie fell back into the present with a low cry.

"Oh wow," she muttered to herself. That was amazing. She was exhausted, sated, and damn well satisfied.

Tom chuckled. Warmth filled her at the sound. She loved it when he laughed. "Feel good?"

"Shit, yeah."

"Language," he warned.

Frankie held back her sigh. She was in too good a mood to

want to ruin it by moaning about his silly rule regarding her swearing.

"I love you, honey. I wish I was there." There was a hint of longing in his voice. She felt a surge of loneliness. What would she do without him?

"I love you too, Tom. I miss you. It's lonely here without you."

"Why don't you go spend tomorrow night with Heath and Anna, honey?" Tom asked with concern.

"Oh no, I'm fine. They're busy preparing for baby number two. I'd just be in the way." And she wasn't in the mood to watch Anna and her brother. She hated herself for it, but she was incredibly jealous of how together Anna was. She was secure in Heath's love and protection. She had Jaron and, even though this pregnancy was putting her through the wringer, soon she'd be bringing another baby into the world.

Frankie was a mess. She didn't like her job. She couldn't get pregnant, and she was constantly worried that one day Tom would wake up and realize she wasn't good enough for him.

"That's not true, honey. Listen to me. End the call then go get cleaned up and I'll ring you back in fifteen."

"It's too early to go to bed, Tom," she whined. She looked at the clock, it wasn't even nine.

"You need an early night," he said sternly. "I can hear the exhaustion in your voice and you've got work tomorrow."

"But I haven't even had dinner." Frankie knew it was a mistake as soon as she'd said it. She wasn't even hungry, she was just trying to delay going to bed.

"You what?" Tom asked her, his voice darkening. Shit. She was in trouble now. "Why not?"

"I was busy," she defended.

"Doing what?"

Yeah, no way was she telling him about the pregnancy test.

"Just stuff," she muttered.

"Not good enough. Were you even going to eat dinner?" he asked intuitively. Damn it. Having a husband who paid attention could have its downside. Especially when said husband believed in spanking.

"Probably not. I hate eating by myself."

"Not a good excuse, Frankie. We're going to have a talk about that when I get home."

Uh oh, she mouthed to herself. She knew what he meant by *talk.* Sure, they'd talk. But the conversation would end with her over his lap getting her ass pounded on.

"You have an hour to make yourself some dinner, get cleaned up and into bed. When I call you, I expect you to be in bed, ready for sleep. Understand?"

"Yes," she said in a subdued voice.

"Oh, and baby? That was super hot. Thank you."

Warmed at his words, she ended the call with a smile.

EXACTLY AN HOUR LATER, Frankie's cell rang.

"Hi, honey," she answered.

"Hi yourself, gorgeous. You in bed?"

"Yes." She snuggled down under the covers with a yawn.

"Good girl. Although I'm still not happy."

She bit her lip. She hated disappointing him. Sometimes she felt like all she did was mess up. She wouldn't blame him if he got tired of her one day. If he left. Her stomach tightened into a knot, the dinner she'd eaten threatening to come back up.

"I need you to take care of yourself while I'm gone, Francesca."

She sniffled. "I'm sorry. I'm worse than a child, aren't I? Well, I guess that's karma. I'm a childish brat who doesn't deserve children and that's why I can't have any. Maybe I should leave and give you a chance to find someone who's not as fucked up as I am."

She froze. She couldn't believe what she'd just said.

"Frankie?" She heard the shock in his voice. "What are you talking about? I cannot believe you just threatened to leave me!"

In a panic, Frankie ended the call, staring at her phone like it was a snake as it rang over and over. Then the landline buzzed. Frankie crawled under the covers, hiding. Stress gnawed at her.

What the hell was wrong with her? She was terrified of Tom leaving her. She couldn't imagine life without him. She'd tried her best to give him everything he might want. She really needed to answer the phone. Apologize. Tell him she didn't mean a word of it. But she found herself frozen. Silence hit her. The phone had stopped ringing.

He'd given up.

Tears welled in her eyes. Idiot. *You wouldn't answer the phone because you didn't want to talk to him and now you're upset because he's given up trying to talk to you? Jesus, Frankie.*

She was an emotional wreck. She was stuck in a downward spiral with no way up. She'd just wanted things to be perfect. To be an amazing wife, to have wonderful babies, to give Tom the life he deserved.

Instead she'd dug herself into a miserable hole and she was only making things worse.

TOM BARELY RESISTED THROWING his phone across the hotel room. Wrecking his phone wasn't going to help or change things. Shit. She didn't actually mean what she said. He knew she didn't. Frankie felt things strongly and she didn't always think before she spoke, which had gotten her into trouble more than once.

But she loved him. Almost as much as he loved her. She'd been under a lot of stress in recent months. She worked too hard. They took advantage of her. He'd been meaning to put his foot down about her job, but it was a tricky situation. He didn't want to control her. Sure, he might be the head of their little household, but only because Frankie gave him that power.

And he'd never abuse it. Never want to push her too hard. All he wanted was her happiness. For her to be healthy and safe. He rubbed his hand over his forehead. He was pretty certain she wasn't going to answer. Just his luck that he was stuck halfway across the country.

He called her one last time, leave a message and then try to get to sleep.

Yeah, like that was going to happen.

2

Frankie stared at the flashing light of the answer machine. She knew the message was from Tom. She swallowed heavily, working up the courage to listen to it. She'd lain awake most of the night, filled with guilt and worry. Why had she said that to him? What had she been thinking?

She hadn't been. She'd been upset over another month passing without getting pregnant. That combined with Tom being away and she'd said something stupid that she now really regretted.

She needed to get ready. If she didn't hurry up, she'd be late for work. Face scrunched up, not really wanting to hear the message, she quickly reached down and pressed the playback button.

Tom's voice immediately came through the speaker, rich and stern.

"Young lady, what rule do we have in our house? If I am calling, you must always pick up. That's two."

She frowned. *Two? What was one?*

As though he could hear her, he continued. "One was not eating dinner. New rule. Never hang up on me in the middle of a conversation. It's disrespectful and rude. And you will not be leaving me. Ever. That was a horrible threat to make. Honey," his voice became quieter, gentler. "I know you're tired. When I get home, we're going to sit down and have a long talk. I don't like seeing you so upset. I'll call you during your lunch hour. Make sure you answer. I love you, baby. Drive safely. Eat. Take care of yourself."

The message ended and it was then she realized she had tears running down her face. What had she ever done to deserve such a man?

BY THE TIME lunchtime came around, Frankie was a nervous wreck. She'd spent most of the morning berating herself. Her boss had even asked her if she was ill and needed to go home. She'd been tempted to lie and say yes, only what would she do at home except obsess more? At least work provided some distraction.

She moved out into the sunshine and found a quiet bench to sit on in the adjacent park to the clinic where she worked.

Her cell rang and Tom's name flashed on the screen. Frankie ran her finger over the screen to unlock her phone, and then drew it up to her ear.

"Hello, honey," she said hesitantly.

"Baby." Tom's voice immediately had tears rising to her eyes. The relief in his tone humbled her and doubled her guilt. "Are you okay? I'm so worried about you."

"I'm sorry." she said with a sniffle. Okay, she needed to get herself under control. She couldn't burst into tears right now. "I don't know what's wrong with me. I just couldn't talk to you again last night. I didn't really mean that stuff about leaving you."

God, she would be lost without Tom.

"I know you didn't, honey. But saying you're going to leave me, even in the heat of the moment, is serious. I stressed all last night that you were packing your bags. That you wouldn't be there when I got home. Do you know how frightened I was? No more ignoring my calls, got it? I can't function with worrying that something has happened to you. I even looked up flights last night to see if I could get one home early."

Now she felt even worse. He'd been looking forward to this conference for months. "No, please, don't do that. I'm fine. I just miss you and I was already upset last night..." she trailed off.

"Why were you so upset?" Tom asked her quietly.

"Well, I—" Crap. What was she going to tell him? She couldn't lie but she didn't want to tell him the truth, knowing the trouble it would get her in.

"Frankie, you know you can tell me anything, don't you?"

"You're going to be mad at me."

He sighed. "Have I ever yelled at you?"

"No."

"Hit you? And we both know I'm not talking about a spanking."

"No, you'd never hit me." Ever. Spanking her was something completely different. She knew some people wouldn't always see it like that. But she knew the difference. Tom's spankings were given out of love. They were also something she needed from him. Both of them had agreed that he would be the leader in their little household, and that his discipline was needed when she broke the rules in order to keep her feeling safe. She felt better when she had boundaries.

"Are you scared of me?"

"No, of course I'm not."

"Do you want to revisit your rules? Or the way our marriage works? Do you regret giving me so much power? You know that ultimately all the power is yours, right? You can always tell me that you want to change things."

"I don't want anything to change, Tom. I love you." Sometimes so much it hurt. And she knew she couldn't keep this from him.

"I took another pregnancy test," she whispered. "It was negative."

There was silence at the other end and for a moment she worried he hadn't heard her. She rubbed at her tummy which was tied in a hard knot.

"I seem to recall forbidding you to do another test without me present."

Frankie remained quiet. She didn't think it was a good idea to point out that she didn't really like the word 'forbid'.

"Baby, why would you do that? You know I don't like you taking them alone because you get so upset. I want to be there to take care of you. To hold you. It kills me how upset you get. Especially when I'm not there to look after you."

"I'm sorry," she said, feeling terrible. "I just couldn't wait."

"I know," he said tenderly. "Frankie, I just want you to be happy. This explains so much about last night. I know how hard this is on you. I wish I was there to hold you. This is going to happen. We'll get pregnant."

"I know," she whispered because she knew it was what he wanted her to say. But she was starting to wonder.

"I love you. It's going to be okay. I'll be home around ten tomorrow morning. Jeff will drop me off. Now, have you had some lunch?"

"Not yet."

"I want you to go and eat some lunch and stop worrying so much. I really think it would be a good idea for you to go stay with Heath and Anna tonight."

"No," she said urgently then tempered her tone. "No, that's okay. I don't feel like company."

"All right. I will call you tonight. Pick up the phone. I love you."

"I love you, too."

. . .

TOM ENDED the call with a frown. Damn, of all the times for him to be away. He could tell how upset his wife was. Her failure to get pregnant was knocking her around.

He wanted children. Eventually. But he wondered now if they would have been better to wait a while before trying to fall pregnant. They'd started soon after getting married. He guessed he'd gotten caught up in the idea and not thought about the reality—about whether they were both truly ready for a baby. They were both young, they had plenty of time.

Tom vowed to pay more care and attention to her. With his practice needing so much time lately, he hadn't been home as much as he would like to. And he was really worried about Frankie.

Not that his wife wasn't a capable, smart woman. She was all those things and more. She was brilliant at her job and he was so proud of her. But she didn't always cope well with stress. She tended to find other outlets to mask the effects stress was having on her, like shopping or throwing herself into her work.

It had been a battle of wills when they were first married. Anytime Frankie got upset, she'd go shopping and rack up a huge bill. And while they were comfortable, she didn't need half the stuff she bought, and if there was one thing Tom hated it was waste.

So each time Frankie went on a stress-related spree, Tom made her return everything then he'd sit her down to have a talk. Which usually led to a trip over his knee. Often it was only during a spanking that Frankie truly let go.

He needed to get to the bottom of what was really going on with her. Both of them needed to take a step back and evaluate what they were doing.

He couldn't lose her. She was his everything.

Tom let out a deep breath. He hated that she'd threatened to disappear on him. Fear pierced his heart at the idea of not having Frankie in his life. He'd loved her since she was a rebellious teenager. It was always Frankie. He'd wanted to race home last night, spank her, then tie her to the bed so she could never leave him. He smiled a little. Tying her to the bed wasn't a bad idea, then he could play with her at will. Torture her to the point of ecstasy over and over.

Tom was a naturally dominant man. His need to care and nurture was tied in with his need to protect. And Frankie came first in his life. He loved caring for her, indulging her where possible, but he also knew she needed boundaries and consequences.

Frankie had grown up in a household where her father was most definitely the head of the household. When Frankie's parents had died, her oldest brother, Heath had taken over as her guardian.

Frankie was full of fun and fire and he never wanted to smother her or put a damper on her spirit. He just wanted to make sure that she had fun while being as safe as possible.

Tom hadn't had much of a home life. His father had left before he'd turned five. When his mother had remarried, he'd been ten. She'd focused all her attention on her new husband. Rod wasn't a bad man, but he'd had his own family from a previous marriage and hadn't been interested in Tom.

Frankie thrived with rules and structure. Maybe he'd been too lenient with her? He hadn't created many rules. He hadn't wanted her to think him overly strict or controlling. But that threat to leave him had him rattled and he couldn't help but think he might be failing her.

What they needed was a holiday. Some time away just the two of them, where he could work on getting Frankie to fully open up with him. The only time she truly let go was when he disciplined her.

He was starting to wonder if she felt just as insecure now as she had when they had first started dating. She was just better at hiding it. And he hated the idea that she thought she had to hide how she truly felt. He needed to spend more time reassuring her of his love.

It was time to fully take charge.

Tom scrolled through the contacts on his phone until he reached Heath's name. His brother-in-law picked up on the fourth ring.

"Hey, Tom, what can I do for you?" Heath's voice was calm, unhurried. Tom admired the man. He was the rock in his family, had been since his parents death. He'd held his family together. Tom knew no matter what else was going on, that any of them—Tom included—could go to him and he'd give them his full attention.

"Hey, Heath. How's it going? How are Anna and Jaron?"

"Jaron's good. Growing fast," Heath said with very real affection for his stepson in his voice. "Running around and getting into mischief. Anna isn't very happy. She wants to be running around after him. I'm not her favorite person at the moment."

"You want me to check up on her?" Tom asked with concern. Anna was nearly five months pregnant and it wasn't going easy on her. Her blood pressure was high, she was excessively tired and having a toddler to chase around wasn't helping matters much.

"That would probably be a good idea. When you have time. Not that she's any worse, but if you could just reiterate the need to rest and not stress. She's pushing me hard. I'm not sure how much stricter I can get with her."

Tom heard the tightness in his voice, knew worry over Anna's health was starting to wear on the stoic man.

"I'll come out some time this week," Tom promised. "I hate to ask, but can you do me a favor?"

"Of course."

"Stop in and check up on Frankie for me tonight. She's a bit upset. I'll be home tomorrow, but..."

"But you're worried about her and you'd feel better if someone checked on her," Heath finished understanding exactly how he felt.

"Yeah," Tom said with relief.

"Of course, I will. She's still my little sister. If I think she needs it, I'll bring her home with me."

"Thanks."

"Hey, no thanks needed. We're family, remember?"

Tom ended the call, feeling much happier.

LATER THAT NIGHT, Tom tiredly climbed the stairs to his hotel room. He was glad that the conference was finally over and he could get home to Frankie tomorrow.

His cell buzzed just as he entered his room. He looked down, hoping to see Frankie's name. Instead it was Heath's.

"Hi, Heath," he answered as he sat on a chair and toed off his shoes.

"Tom."

Tom immediately tensed at the displeasure in Heath's voice.

"What is it? What's happened?" Tom asked urgently.

"I'm at your place. Frankie's not here."

Tom looked over at his clock. Seven forty-five. She should be home by now, even if she'd stopped on the way home to get groceries or takeaways.

"Your house is all locked up and her car isn't in the garage."

"Damn," Tom sighed. "I'm sorry to get you all the way there for nothing. I'll call her cell. She must have gone out to dinner with friends. She'll probably be home soon. She knew I was going to call her." He called at eight each night.

"I'll wait," Heath said.

"No, you need to get home to Anna. I'm sure Frankie's fine. You know how easily she loses track of time."

Heath was quiet. "Are you sure you don't want me to go looking for her?"

"No. Honestly, go home. Thanks, Heath."

"You call me if you need to. Promise."

Tom smiled. Heath sounded like a concerned parent, and he guessed in a way he was. He'd raised Frankie from a teenager.

"I promise."

He closed his phone then rubbed his forehead. A headache was forming in his temples. He'd give her until eight then he'd call. After all, she didn't know he'd asked Heath to come around. Tom hadn't wanted it to look like he was checking up on her when that was exactly what he was doing.

Tom hated that he was miles away from her right now. Not when she was hurting, confused. The fact that she wasn't safely tucked up inside their house ate at him. Especially after her threat to leave him.

He paced. Fifteen minutes had never seemed so long.

Seven fifty-eight. Close enough.

Tom called the house phone. It rang until the answer phone picked up. Letting out a deep breath in an attempt to cage his fear, he called her cell. No answer.

"God damn it, Frankie," he swore. "I'm going to whip your butt good for scaring me like this."

He called the house phone then her cell again, leaving messages on both.

Sitting back on the bed, he prepared himself for a long night.

Where the hell was she?

∾

WHAT WAS SHE DOING HERE?

Frankie stared around her with blurry eyes as she sat in the crowded nightclub. She'd only intended to go out to dinner with her workmates. They'd begged her to join them and she'd given in. She hated eating alone. Instead of driving home to Hammersly to change, she'd showered at Libby's house, borrowing some of her clothes.

Unfortunately, Libby was a bit smaller than Frankie, so a top that looked fairly good on Libby was basically obscene on Frankie. At the restaurant, she'd kept her jacket on to cover herself up, but it was too hot inside the club to keep it on.

After having a few drinks with dinner, it hadn't taken much for the others to persuade her to come here, but she really wished she hadn't. Tom was going to kill her. Not that he would have stopped her from going out, but she was supposed to tell him where she was going and with who so he knew she was safe. Oh shit. He would have called at eight and she'd turned off her phone!

Why was she acting this way? She wasn't even enjoying herself. She felt nauseous from a combination of guilt and alcohol. She was exhausted. Her feet hurt from being stuffed into Libby's too-small high heels and she'd been hit on so many times, she'd lost count. She'd actually had to stomp her heel down on one guy's foot just to get him to back off.

He was none too pleased either. Even now, he stood glaring at her from across the room.

It was time to leave. She had to call Tom. She had no idea what time it was, but she could only imagine how mad he was. And worried.

She was in big trouble.

Heaving herself up, she swayed as she attempted to search out her friends. Dragging out her cell, she nearly threw as she tried to read the screen.

This wasn't good. How was she going to get home?

She could take a taxi but it would cost a fortune. There was no way she could drive. Not in this condition. Pulling off her shoes, she held them in one hand, her cell clutched tightly in her other hand as she pushed and shoved her way to the door.

Stumbling out the door, she took in deep gulps of cold air.

Shivering, she glanced down at herself in confusion.

"Damn, where is my jacket?" she muttered. Where had she put her it? Did she leave it in the club? She must have.

"I need to go back inside," she muttered, shivering. But as she turned she saw that guy from earlier. The one who hadn't understood the word no. He glared at her.

Yeah, probably time to leave. She weaved her way down the pavement. Maybe she could call one of her brothers. Hmm...who would scold her the least? She looked over her shoulder. Oh shit, creepy guy was still following her. Fear made her heart race and she turned to run right as she smashed into someone. Two hands grasped hold of her arms as she wobbled, nearly falling on her butt. She gasped with fright.

"Are you all right?" a deep voice asked.

Frankie glanced up at the smartly-dressed man in front of her. His dark hair gleamed under the streetlight, his tanned skin a nice contrast to the white shirt he wore tucked into black pants. She took a step back nervously, although she didn't get a creepy vibe like she did from that other ass. She looked back over her shoulder.

"He's gone," the dark-haired man said.

"Who?" She whipped her head back, wincing as it started to throb. Not a smart move.

"The male who was following you. I take it he wasn't a friend of yours."

"Hardly. Just some idiot who doesn't understand the word no."

"It's not safe for you to be walking around on your own in the dark. And why aren't you wearing shoes? There could be glass on the ground."

"I know that," she said defensively, even though she hadn't really considered that at all.

"What are you doing out here on your own, little one?"

She stared up at him. "First of all, I'm hardly little. Secondly, what business is it of yours if I'm wandering around alone?"

His gaze narrowed and she shivered a little at the look of displeasure on his face. Okay, this was a guy who was used to being in command.

"I was walking to my car when I saw you weave your way out of that nightclub, shoes in hand. Then I saw that man exit and start to follow you. So I thought I better see if you were in trouble."

She swallowed nervously. Maybe she should be thanking this guy rather than bitching at him.

"Okay, well, thank you. I appreciate the help. I'm going home now."

"How are you getting home?" he asked. "Do you need me to call you a taxi?"

She shook her head, groaning as that made it throb mercilessly. She really wanted to go home. To her own bed. And sleep forever. "No thanks. No taxi. Too expensive. I live in Hammersly."

He frowned. "Can I give you a ride home then?"

"I'm fine. I'm going to call my brother. One of them. Brax probably, he'll be less likely to spank me."

Oops, had she said that out loud? She smacked her hand across her mouth.

The man laughed. There was something about him. He kind of reminded her of Tom. That tone of voice that brooked no argument, the way he held himself.

"You're shivering. I wish I had a jacket to give you."

"That's okay. I had one. Guess it's lost now." Frankie closed her eyes briefly, wobbling. "Whoa."

Suddenly she found propped up with a firm arm around her waist. Her face buried against a warm chest.

"Easy, little one. I won't hurt you. You were about to fall over."

She took a shuddering breath as she realized he'd tucked her in against him.

"Oh, thanks. You can let me go."

He slowly stepped back, his arm outstretched as though to catch her if she fell. "Now tell me where you live or give me your brother's number and I'll ring him. Did you say his name was Brax? I know a Brax Jamieson, is that him?"

"How do you know him?" she asked suspiciously.

"I've met him a few times. So what's it going to be, little one?" he said in a tone of voice she knew well. "Am I calling Brax or giving you a ride home because I am not leaving you out here. You're in no condition to look after yourself. You need a spanking for this little stunt."

Frankie groaned. "Not you, too. Don't worry. I'm sure my husband will take care of it when he gets home tomorrow."

"Yeah? And who is he?"

"Tom Sanders," she replied tiredly. She should probably resist him, but she really wanted to sleep.

"That so?" he said, his voice amused for some reason. "Well, can't let Doc Sanders wife stand around in the cold, can I?"

"You know Tom?" she asked.

"I knew him years ago." He glanced down at her feet. "You can't walk around in bare feet."

"They're too sore to put my shoes back on."

"I'll carry you then."

Before she could reply, she was in the air. She found herself cradled against a warm, firm chest. Her stomach rolled at the sudden movement. He started walking.

"I'm surprised your husband let you go out this late without him." They reached a dark car and he set her down then opened the door. What were the odds of meeting a guy who knew Brax and Tom? He helped her inside and pulled the belt across her.

Frankie frowned. "I'm not a child."

The car started moving and she closed her eyes, hoping that would help the nausea. "You deserve a damn good spanking for this. I'm half tempted to do it myself."

"What is it with the men around here?" she complained. "All you ever do is spank and scold."

He snorted. "You're obviously married to the wrong man if that's all he does, sweetheart."

She sighed. "More like he's married to the wrong woman."

"I find that hard to believe."

A sob escaped. "I can't have children."

A warm hand encased hers. "I'm sorry, sweetheart. Did you just find out?"

"We've been trying for a year and nothing. He deserves better. He needs a wife who can give him the perfect life." Part of her was horrified that she was blurting this all out to a stranger. That she had even accepted a ride with him was bad enough, she didn't need to tell him all her secrets too.

"No such thing as perfect. If all he wants from you are children then he doesn't deserve to have you."

She sniffled miserably.

"Is that why you were out getting drunk tonight?"

Maybe it was the alcohol reducing her inhibitions or that she just needed to tell someone, but Frankie found herself confessing everything. Her pain over another failed pregnancy test. The fact that she thought Tom would be better off without her. Her failure to be the perfect wife.

When she finished, she realized he'd stopped the car and was holding her against his chest as she cried.

"Oh my God, I'm so sorry," she apologized, mortified. She moved back to her own seat, wiping her hands over her cheeks.

"Don't be. Sounds to me like you needed to get that all off your chest. Sometimes it's easier to talk to someone you don't know. Someone that has no investment in your life."

"I feel like all I ever do is cause him trouble. What do I ever give back?"

"Ahh, sweetheart, I'm sure you give plenty. And if he wants more, then your husband seems like a man who will let you know."

She frowned. Her alcohol buzz had long died. Now she just felt sick and tired. "I don't know, sometimes I feel like he holds back."

He kissed her forehead. "Talk to him. He will listen. Here, if you ever need someone to talk to, come and see me." He drew back and pulled out his wallet, handing her a card. "You call me any time you need to talk, okay?"

She clutched the card and nodded.

He started the car again. "Let's get you home. It's well past your bedtime, little one."

Feeling subdued and thoroughly exhausted, Frankie gave him directions. This was turning into one hell of a night.

3

Tom waved goodbye to Jeff before striding up the walkway to his house, pulling his suitcase behind him. He quickly unlocked the door. As soon as he was inside, he dropped the case and started striding up the stairs, pushing back the exhaustion weighing him down.

He hadn't been able to sleep last night; his worry over Frankie kept him awake, fearing the worse. He prayed to God he'd find her safe and sound in their bed. Nearly too afraid to look in case he found the room empty, Tom slowly pushed their bedroom door open.

And nearly collapsed in relief.

She was sound asleep, dressed in clothes that weren't hers, but she was there.

"Thank you, God," he whispered, running his hand over his face. Part of him wanted to immediately shake her awake, hug her, scold her, then spank her ass red. And then start all over again. But he knew he had to get some sleep, get himself under control. He was so tired and angry that he was concerned about what he'd say in this state.

As he walked towards her, the smell of alcohol hit him and he grimaced. He ran his gaze over her. She wore a too-small top, her breasts nearly bursting out of the sequined top. A short skirt had ridden right up her legs until he could see her bare ass, the tiny G-string doing little to cover her. Normally, he loved those tiny scraps of lingerie she wore, but he wondered how many people had seen her butt in that pathetic excuse for a skirt.

Tom was a possessive man and he wasn't apologetic about that fact. What was his, was his. As caveman as that sounded.

Her dark, normally silken hair lay tangled and messy around her head and her mouth was open as she snored softly. Mascara was smeared under her eyes and there were smudges of red on the pillowcase from her lipstick.

"Obviously someone had a good night while I was worrying myself sick," he muttered.

Taking a deep breath to cool his ire, Tom turned to move towards the attached bathroom. He needed a shower then a long sleep.

Something caught his eye on the floor. Bending down, he picked up a white business card. He frowned, staring at his wife in shock. His gut clenched tight, a sick feeling developing. Where the hell had she gotten this from? Just what had she gotten up to last night?

One thing was for certain. When his wife woke up, she was in a hell of a lot of trouble.

FRANKIE GROANED, her head pounding incessantly, her mouth hellishly dry. She placed her arm over her eyes, hoping to hide from the world. Why? Why did she drink so much last night? It never ended up good the next day. Her stomach rolled and she willed the urge to vomit away.

Not good. Really not good.

"Finally, she joins the land of the living."

She gasped, opening her eyes, her gaze immediately focusing in on her husband who was sitting in an armchair by the window. He stared back at her solemnly. He looked tired, unhappy.

"Tom? When did you get home?" she asked. She sat up slowly, trying to hide her wince of pain as her head throbbed. The room spun and she had to take slow, shallow breaths to stop herself from vomiting. Her bra dug into her side. Why hadn't she taken her clothes off last night? She hated sleeping in her bra.

Tom glanced at the clock on her side table. "About four hours ago."

"What?" Frankie stared at the clock in shock, realizing it was now two pm. "I-I—"

"You what?" he asked calmly, his voice flat, emotionless.

Something was very, very wrong.

Of course, something is wrong, idiot.

She'd spent last night drinking and partying. She'd turned off her phone. Fallen asleep in these god-awful clothes, probably smelling like a brewery. And then she hadn't even woken up when her husband got home.

Wow. Wife of the year.

"I'm sorry I wasn't awake when you got home," she said, trying to gauge just how angry he was. His face remained impassive, although she swore she saw his eyes flash.

"Really? Out of all the things you could apologize for that's what you're going to go with?" he asked coolly.

Frankie bit her lip. She rubbed her head, trying to ease the pain.

Tom rose and walked into the bathroom. He returned minutes later with a glass of water. He passed it to her, as well as some painkillers before returning to his chair.

"Thanks," she murmured, tears welling in her eyes. Had she

behaved so horribly that he couldn't even bring himself to hug her? To give her a kiss?

"Where were you last night, Frankie?" he asked. "I called you. Heath came around to check up on you. I had no idea where you were. If you were safe. I was awake all night worrying about you. And it seems you were off partying and having a good time."

She winced. Misery enveloped her. What a fuck-up she was. "I'm so sorry. I went out for dinner with some friends from work and one thing sort of led to another and we ended up at a nightclub."

"And it didn't occur to you to let me know? That when I couldn't get hold of you I would worry? Do you realize how terrified I was, Frankie? Wondering where you were? If you were hurt? If someone had attacked you? Raped you? Killed you? What were you thinking? How hard would it have been to answer your phone or send me a text to let me know you were okay?"

Guilt raged as she listened to him scold, still in that awful flat voice, his disappointment in her clear to see.

"I know, you're right, but—"

"No buts, no excuses. You were already in trouble for hanging up on me. Then you blatantly disrespected me and our relationship again by disappearing without telling me where you were going. Without even sending me a simple text so I didn't worry. I don't know how I'm supposed to trust you, Frankie."

His disappointment in her was like daggers wounding her.

Tom sighed. "What's going on, Frankie? You know you can tell me anything, right?"

But how did she tell him that she was worried he'd one day realized she was more trouble than she was worth? Was she trying to sabotage her relationship? Or was she acting out to get his attention? That thought made her feel ill. She hadn't done it consciously. It was immature and foolish.

Shit.

"I know," she whispered.

He gave her a knowing look. "I am going to get to the bottom of all of this. You're not acting like yourself. I know not getting pregnant is wearing on you, sweetheart. We need to talk about that too."

What did that mean?

Tom held up a card. It was the one that man had given her last night.

"Where did you get this from, Frankie?" he asked, his voice as cold as she'd ever heard it.

She swallowed heavily.

"Think very hard about your answer, because it had better be the truth. I suggest you start at the beginning, tell me everything, including where you got those atrocious clothes from."

He'd been angry at her before, but he'd never been like this— so very tight and controlled.

"My workmates wanted me to go out for dinner with them. I didn't want to drive all the way home and then back, so a workmate lent me some of her clothes."

He gave the clothing in question a disparaging look.

"After dinner, they wanted to go for a drink. I shouldn't have gone, but they were insistent. I'm sorry."

He sighed. "I'm not upset because you went out with your workmates, Frankie. I'm upset because you didn't tell me. Because you turned off your phone. Because I had no idea if you were all right. How did you get home? Please don't tell me you drove."

She was shocked he would even ask her that. "No, of course not. I got a ride."

"In a taxi?"

"No, I wouldn't spend so much money on a taxi. I promise."

"Francesca, I'm not worried about how much money you spent. I'm worried about whether you were safe. Now, who did you get a ride with?"

This was the part she really didn't want to tell him. She still couldn't believe she'd done what she had. What had she been thinking?

She hadn't been thinking.

"I got a ride home from the guy who gave me that card," she said in a small voice.

He stiffened.

"He said he knew Brax. And you."

"And you took him at his word?"

How did she describe that there was something about him that had just inspired confidence?

"You let a man you didn't know drive you home just because he said he knew your brother? He could have been anyone! He could have been a murderer or a rapist. He could have taken you anywhere."

"When you put it like that it doesn't sound so good."

"No, it really doesn't. Why didn't you call one of your brothers?"

"I was going to. Then he turned up." She realized she didn't even know his name. She hadn't actually looked at the card Tom still held in his hand.

"Nothing like that happened, though. He wasn't a crazy killer or anything."

"But you didn't know that!" he nearly yelled, shocking her. Tom never raised his voice.

"You were completely vulnerable. I don't know what to do about this, Frankie. I don't know how to instill in you a sense of self-preservation. I need to make sure this never happens again, but I..." he trailed off, just shaking his head. "I really don't know what to do. I need some time to think."

Fear churned in her already nauseous stomach. She hated that she'd disappointed him. Hated that he sounded so uncertain. Tom always knew what to do. Ignoring her queasy stomach and throbbing headache, she climbed out of the bed and walked over to kneel at his feet. She leaned her forehead in his lap.

"Please, Tom. Please."

She didn't want a rift between them. And she never wanted to make him regret choosing her. Marrying her.

"Please, what?" he asked.

"Please punish me," she begged. She never thought she'd actually beg to be spanked. "I want to make this right."

"I don't know if you can."

She shook, sobbing. No, please God, no. She couldn't bear it if he gave up on her. "Y-you're leaving me?"

"Christ." He grabbed her under the arms and lifted her onto his lap. "Of course I'm not leaving you."

Tears dripped down her face as she shuddered. She felt so cold, even with him holding her tight.

Tom tucked her head against his chest, holding her close as he rocked her gently. She cried, burying her face into his chest. This was her worst nightmare, losing him. If he'd just give her another chance, she'd make things better. She'd do anything she had to.

"Hey, baby. Come on. I didn't mean to scare you. Stop crying, please. You know I hate it when you cry."

"S-sorry," she hiccupped, trying to get herself under control.

He pulled her back so he could stare at her. He wiped his thumb over each cheek. "Listen to me well. I love you. I am not ever leaving you. Even when you mess up."

"Even if it happens a lot?"

He grinned for the first time since he got back. "Even then."

"I'm so sorry, Tom. For everything. I hate when I disappoint you."

"All I want is for you to be happy and safe, Frankie. You scared me. I can't lose you."

"I can't lose you either." She had to do better. "I love you."

"I love you as well." He kissed her gently then wrinkled his nose. "You do smell like a brewery, though."

She grimaced. "Sorry."

He ran his hand over her hair. "The last two nights I sat up worrying about you, scared you were in trouble and I couldn't help you. I can't experience that again."

Frankie nodded, taking a big breath. She knew what needed to happen. "You should spank me." At least then it would be over and he would forgive

Tom chuckled, surprising her. When she glanced up at him, though, his face was solemn. "Oh honey, this is going to be much harder than a simple spanking."

Oh, wonderful.

"I am seriously worried about you. And I need to do whatever is necessary to ensure this doesn't happen again."

Frankie gulped.

He cupped her chin in his palm, raising her face so she stared into his dark eyes. "You know I only do this because I love you and because I believe you need this, for me to take charge. You're not scared of me, are you?"

"No." She shook her head, shocked that he'd think that. "Never. When you use that voice on me, the one that tells me you're in charge now, my stomach drops and a kind of peace comes over me. I guess because I know you're in control and I trust you to take care of me. I don't have to worry, because you'll be there to look after me."

She buried her face against him in embarrassment. He kissed her forehead, rubbing her back soothingly.

"Thank you for being so honest, baby. I know that wasn't easy. I never want you to forget and that is that I love you and want to protect you. Never forget that."

"I love you, too," she whispered.

He kissed her. "It's settled then. But first, there's a question I need to ask. I want an honest answer. Do you know just who gave you a ride home last night?"

TOM WAITED FOR HER REPLY, praying she had no idea who the man who'd driven her home was. Because if she did, if she'd lied and betrayed him... well, he had no idea what he would do.

"No. I'm sorry," she said quickly, obviously thinking he'd be furious at her answer. "I know I shouldn't have gotten a ride with someone I didn't know. But he said he knew Brax and you, and he was willing to wait with me while I called him. I just... I know there are no excuses. But his name must be on the card he gave me. I guess I should call him and thank him."

"No," he said sharply. Frankie jumped in his arms, looking at him with wide, frightened eyes. Tom squashed his anger.

"I don't want you anywhere near this guy. Understand?"

Frankie gaped at him. "Why? Is he dangerous?"

"I wouldn't put it past him to orchestrate a meeting with you so I would have to see him again."

Rage filled his veins. His hands clenched, his jaw tensing. A soft hand ran over his face, trying to soothe him.

"Tom? Who is he?"

"Who he is isn't important. Just stay away from him, hear me?"

4

Frankie dressed slowly. She couldn't believe Tom had left. Well, he'd made her some breakfast which she'd taken a few bites of to satisfy him. Then he'd run her a bath, even helping her bathe, which had been more of a curse than a help. His touch had heat surging through her body, which unfortunately he'd done nothing to ease.

He'd refused to tell her anything more about the man who had given her a ride home last night. Even though it was obvious there was something going on. He'd gotten a cold, stubborn look on his face that she'd rarely seen on him before. And she hadn't wanted to press him. Not when they were already on shaky ground.

She'd expected him to punish her after getting her out of the bath. Instead he'd dressed her in one of her nightgowns and put her back to bed.

Then he'd left!

She'd lain in bed for a while, unable to sleep, her brain going over and over everything. She felt anxious and unsettled. Especially since he'd left without punishing her and making things right.

She didn't even know where he'd gone. Although he'd taken that card with him. So she guessed maybe it had something to do with the guy from last night. Who was he? What did he mean to Tom?

Unable to take the questions in her head anymore, she'd decided to get up and dressed. She needed some fresh air. And some perspective.

TOM STOOD in the foyer of Indulgence, waiting for Roarke to appear. He'd been told to take a seat, but he was feeling too restless to sit. Instead, he stared around at the richly-appointed greeting area. Roarke always had impeccable taste.

He knew the other man would see him. He wouldn't be able to resist. Tom was impatient, though. He was starting to regret leaving Frankie as he had. He hadn't really gotten to the bottom of what was truly going on with her. And he hadn't settled things between them. If he hadn't been so upset by Roarke's reappearance, he wouldn't have left as he had. The fact that Roarke had approached Frankie had rattled him.

He needed to get back to her. Now.

"Tom, I thought you might visit."

Tom glanced up and looked at the man he'd once considered to be a brother. He looked older, but on him, the extra lines on his face only made him look more distinguished. His blue eyes studied Tom calmly as he leaned against a doorway, arms crossed loosely over his large chest.

Damn, he was still a big, muscular bastard.

"You going to continue to stare at me all afternoon or would you like to come inside?"

With a snort Tom started forward, following Roarke as he turned and walked down the passage behind him.

"Indulgence is a bit of a cliché name, don't you think?" Tom sneered, while inwardly he winced. One minute in this man's presence and he was reduced to a rebellious teen. Where was all his control?

Roarke just looked over his shoulder at him coolly. "It fits the club. People come here to indulge their fantasies." He led Tom into an empty bar. It was dark—black tables, black furniture and fixtures. The only color was dark maroon carpet and drapes.

"Jesus," Tom muttered.

"Something wrong?" Roarke asked with what looked like amusement in his eyes. "You don't like the furnishings?"

"Like I said before, clichéd. Don't you have anything original in here?" Tom challenged. On the one hand, he was a bit appalled at his behavior. But the other part of him didn't care.

This was the bastard who'd taken his best friend from him. And Tom would never forget him for that.

Roarke moved behind the bar. "I give people what they expect. This club isn't as hardcore as some of my other clubs. We have open nights a few times a week and run training classes. Drink?"

Tom sneered. "Well, aren't you Mr. Wonderful? Still helping out all the little newbie Doms. Tell me, does it help you sleep better?"

Roarke looked at him calmly. "No, it doesn't. Nothing helps me sleep. All I see when I close my eyes is my little brother racing out the door, knowing I can't stop him. Knowing what happens next. How are your dreams?"

Tom was surprised at the pain in Roarke's eyes. He knew the other man must be suffering, but his own anger had suppressed any empathy for Roarke. He wanted that anger, needed it.

Because he needed someone else to blame. He couldn't carry it all himself. It would drown him.

"I didn't come here to talk about sleeping patterns. I came here to tell you to stay away from my wife."

Roarke raised an eyebrow. "She was a woman alone outside a club, looking distressed. You expected me to just leave her there?"

Tom fought hard to maintain his anger. "You knew she was my wife, didn't you?"

"Yes, I did."

"You had no business approaching her. Were you hoping to use her to get to me?"

Roarke eyed him. "Well, if I had it's worked, hasn't it? Because here you are, filled with righteous anger. I didn't search your wife out. I was merely in the right place at the right time."

"I don't want to see you or talk to you. I am not going to forgive you." Even as he said the words, pain bloomed. He'd held onto his anger for so long, but now faced with Roarke, he remembered the anguish and horror on the other man's face as they'd heard about Austin's accident. Seen him cry after making the decision to turn off the life support. Tom had blocked all that out in his need to blame the other man. "Stay away from her. I catch you near her and I will call the cops. She'll be under orders to do the same."

"But will she obey you?" Roarke asked softly as Tom turned to leave.

Tom turned back. "Yes."

Roarke raised a brow in that infuriatingly superior way he had. "Really? So she had permission to be out at that nightclub on her own? While you were away? With no plan to get home? You allow your sub a lot more leniency than I thought you would."

"She's not my sub, she's my wife."

"She can be both," Roarke told him with amusement. Damn him.

"Well, she's not." Frankie submitted to him when it came to her health and safety. Although, submitted might be too strong a word. She knew if she broke the rules, he'd blister her butt. Whether she obeyed was up to her and her wish to sit for the next week.

"Do you think that's wise? She clearly needs a guiding hand. She's pushing herself so hard that she's self-destructing."

Tom ground his teeth. "What the hell do you know about it?"

"I know that she feels like she has to be this perfect wife, or what she thinks a perfect wife should be. She's trying so hard to be everything she thinks you need, a wife, a housekeeper, a mother, that she's nearly exhausted herself. It's no wonder she went off the rails, she's wound up tighter than a jack-in-the-box."

Tom gaped at him. He'd spoken to Frankie for less than an hour and he'd discovered all that? Tom had been married to her for nearly a year and he was only just coming to realize how insecure she still was in their marriage.

"She told you all that?"

Roarke nodded. "She was rather upset. She needed someone to talk to. She should have come to you, but she's terrified of scaring you off. You need to show her that no matter what you'll be there for her."

Anger suffused him. Most of it aimed at himself, but some spilled over onto the smug bastard before him.

He pointed at Roarke. "Stay out of my life and away from my wife."

"I'm worried about her," Roarke told him, as though he'd known Frankie for years. "When I saw her outside that club she could barely stand."

Although there was no discernible criticism in his voice or face, Tom winced at his words. "Well, by the time I'm through with her, she will regret every moment of it. She won't be sitting comfortably for quite a while."

"Ahh, well, I see you haven't given everything up that I taught you."

Tom flushed a bit. "She responds best when she has boundaries and structure."

"You could bring her here. Train her."

"No." Tom looked around him. "I never truly enjoyed any of this. I kept coming back for Austin. And this is definitely not the place for Frankie."

He meant it. He didn't need to bring Frankie here or to another club. In fact, the idea of others seeing her, watching her, it filled him with possessive jealousy.

She was his.

That didn't mean he didn't recognize his need for control. Frankie functioned better with him in charge. He remembered what she said about feeling safer when he took control. Maybe he needed to set firmer boundaries. It was obvious she was holding things back from him. He needed her to confide in him. To come to him when she had problems, rather than bottling them and then doing something crazy when it all became too much.

"Do you know why I approached Frankie?" Roarke asked. "I was checking out the club as a favor to a friend. I knew she was your wife, so I felt some obligation to look out for her. Some asshole was following her, he was almost on her. I got to her first, luckily, or I'm not sure what would have happened. I suggest you start keeping a closer watch on your wife."

The last sentence was said coldly. Tom glared at him.

"Thank you for giving my wife a ride home, now stay the fuck away from her," he told Roarke hotly before storming out of the club.

5

Frankie watched the horses in the corral, not sure what the hell she was doing here at Heath's ranch. She should be home, waiting for Tom to return. But each time she'd shut her eyes, she'd felt confused and a bit insecure. She couldn't get rid of that voice telling her that one day she was going to lose Tom.

What was wrong with her? This wasn't just about her inability to get pregnant, although that was probably what had stirred all these insecurities up. Tom wasn't going to be happy with her for leaving the house. She'd text him where she was, though. She was tired of thinking. She just wanted to be for a while.

Two horses pranced around, one a dark, deep black with just a white splash between its eyes. That was Anna's mare, Slinky. Weird name for a beautiful horse. The other horse was larger, a stallion with a deep brown coat. Rocky. Both were stunning animals. "Want to go for a ride?"

She turned towards her oldest brother. Tall, broad, his long body encased in well-worn shirt and jeans, a hat hiding his dark hair, Heath was a handsome man. Strong, smart and reliable.

Tears welled. Shit, she was emotional at the moment. It really sucked.

Frankie shook her head.

Heath smiled slightly. "Is that because your butt is too sore or you just don't feel like a ride?"

Frankie's gaze narrowed, the tears disappearing. "What the hell do you know about the state of my ass?"

Heath's face grew stern before he moved to lean against the corral beside her. "Watch your language, and I know you didn't tell Tom you were going out last night."

She sighed. "I'm sorry I wasn't there when you called around." She would have been had she known.

"I should have called you first, there's no need to apologize. To *me*."

"I've apologized to Tom."

Heath clasped her chin lightly, raising her face so she was staring into his eyes. He looked down at her gently, with such understanding that she almost started crying again.

Goddamn it.

"I know that it can be hard living with a husband or brothers like you have," he began.

"What? Ones who like to beat my ass?" she interrupted, wishing back the words as soon as she said them.

"I was going to say overprotective and bossy, before I was so rudely interrupted."

She flushed at the gentle reprimand.

"Sorry," she told him. "I'm a bit out of sorts at the moment." In truth, she liked the fact that her family cared so much for her. She knew so many people who barely even talked to their family. Sure, her brothers and Tom could be arrogant and bossy, and it was embarrassing to still be spanked at her age, but Frankie honestly wouldn't have it any other way.

She knew she was loved. She knew there would always be

someone there for her if she needed them. And she knew no matter what she did, they'd stick by her.

It was no coincidence that she'd fallen in love with a man like her brothers. Although, she'd had a crush on him as a kid, it was only once he'd shown her that he could take charge and would do whatever he thought necessary to protect and care for her, that she'd actually fallen in love with him.

Frankie wouldn't have her life any other way.

She leaned against his wide shoulder. No matter what, she knew she could find some peace here. It was home.

"Does Tom know you're here, sweetheart?" Heath asked kindly.

She sighed. "I texted him."

"What's the matter, baby? You haven't been yourself in a while. You look tired. Pale."

"I'm so confused," Frankie cried. "I don't even know what to do anymore. Nothing is happening the way it is supposed to and I don't know what I'm doing."

Heath pulled her into his arms. "For all your crazy ways at time, you always did like structure. Remember when you were a kid, you used to copy Mom, both of you had lists for everything. You even had a master list for your lists."

Frankie pulled back to look up at him incredulously. "Really?"

"Really," he confirmed. "Of course, your list consisted of all your toys, then there was one of all your friends, and I think yet another of everything you disliked about your smelly, horrible brothers." He smiled.

Frankie scrunched her nose. "I was an awful sister, it's a wonder you put up with me."

Heath frowned and clasped her face in his hands. "No, you weren't. What are you talking about? You were a wonderful sister. I remember once, I came home from a rodeo with a bruised face and a large gash on my leg. You burst into tears and ran out of the room when you saw me. I thought you were going to your bedroom to hide. Instead you came back with the doctor's kit I'd gotten you for Christmas and proceeded to bandage me up. You even kissed my owie to make it all better."

Frankie blushed. "Heath, I was like eight! I'm talking about later, after Mom and Dad died. I was horrid."

"You were a teenage girl whose parents had just died. The life you knew didn't exist anymore and you were lost. Like I said before, honey, you don't deal well without some sort of structure. Of course, you were acting out, you had all these emotions you couldn't deal with, your world was shattered and you were just looking for an anchor to help you. I should have realized earlier. If anything, I was at fault not you."

"It wasn't your fault!" She gaped at him in shock. "You were wonderful. Other brothers probably would have pawned me off on someone else. You gave up your life for me."

Heath grasped hold of her shoulders, shaking her slightly. "No. I do not want you feeling guilty, understand me? You are my sister, I love you, and I would never give you up. My life was exactly what I wanted. You know I like taking care of other people. I have never regretted for one moment taking on this ranch and you. You mean the world to me, kid. I love you."

"I love you, too," she told him. "Thank you for looking after me, for never giving up."

He kissed the top of her forehead. "You're welcome." He pulled back again, staring down at her seriously. "Is everything okay with you and Tom?"

"I love Tom, he's everything to me. I just worry sometimes."

Heath just stared down at her. "About what?"

She shrugged. "Lots of stuff."

"You don't have to tell me, sweetie. But if you ever want to, you know my door is always open."

A heavy weight unraveled in her chest at the acceptance in his gaze. "Thanks, big brother."

"Now, I just put Anna down for a nap and you look like you could use one too. Come on."

Heath held out his hand and she took it with an exasperated sigh. Seemed like everyone was trying to put her to bed today. She'd just come from bed, even though she hadn't gotten any rest. "I can judge when I need to go to bed, you know. So can Anna."

Heath shot her a smile over his shoulder. "Really? Honey, you're so tired you can barely stand without swaying. Anna fought me tooth and nail about a nap then fell asleep as soon as her head hit the pillow. Besides, if you two always had the sense to do what was good for you, who would I fuss over?"

Frankie just shook her head, a smile twitching at her lips.

"You are a bit of a mother hen."

Heath threw back his head and laughed. Delighted she'd managed to make her usually solemn brother laugh, Frankie followed him without protest.

TOM PULLED into his brother-in-law's driveway. He had seen Frankie's text after leaving Indulgence. Coming out to the ranch had been the last thing he'd wanted to do, but he knew Frankie often came home when she was feeling unsure about things. It was the source of that uncertainty that worried him. He needed to get to the bottom of what was going on with his wife.

Sighing tiredly, he pulled his car to a stop outside the sprawling ranch house. He was exhausted. Physically and emotionally.

Seeing Roarke had taken a lot out of him. All he'd wanted was to drive home and hold his wife, reassure himself that she was all right.

The front door opened and Frankie's oldest brother stepped out. Moving forward to lean against the porch post at the top of the stairs, Heath just stared at him.

Tom undid his seatbelt, opened the door and slowly got out.

"Afternoon," Heath called out.

"Hey," Tom greeted him. He followed the other man into the house then to Heath's study. Tom barely bit back a groan. It was a well-known fact that when Heath wanted a "talk" he went to his study. Tom really didn't need a lecture right now.

"Sit down," Heath told him, moving to his alcohol cabinet. "Do you want a drink?"

Tom sat. He was tempted to just close his eyes and sleep. "Better not."

Heath poured himself some whiskey then sat in one of the leather, oversized armchairs Anna had given him for his birthday. They were a gorgeous chocolate color and suited the room, and the man, well.

Tom looked at his brother-in-law, wondering how he did it. He wore his authority like a second skin. He ran a successful ranch. No one ever doubted Heath's authority or challenged him.

"What are you thinking?" Heath asked.

"That anyone would have to be an idiot to challenge you and I'm wondering how I can develop some of your authority," Tom said candidly.

Heath nearly choked on a swallow of whiskey. He patted his chest a few times, his eyes watering. "You think no one ever challenges me? Have you met my wife? Hell, have you met yours?"

Tom waved his hand. "Frankie may have rebelled as a teenager, but she wouldn't dare go against you now. And Anna is a sweet, gentle woman, I'm sure she never gives you any trouble."

Heath grinned. "Well, you'd lose that bet. Frankie loves nothing more than to push me. As for Anna, hell, that woman challenges me all the time. She may come across as sweet, but if she doesn't want to do something I want her to, then she becomes a stubborn brat." Heath smiled. "I wouldn't have it any other way."

Tom sighed. "I've always looked at you and been so jealous. You and Anna, you have it so together, with Frankie I always feel like I'm feeling my way in the dark. I'm worried I'm going to make a mistake and turn her against me."

"And that is your problem," Heath said.

"What?"

"Do you think I don't worry? When my parents died I was terrified about the ranch failing. About taking care of Frankie. My brothers, too. Even though they were grown they still needed me for reassurance, guidance. I had no idea what I was doing. All I knew was what I'd observed and learned from my parents."

"You never showed it," Tom said in shock. Heath always seemed so confident.

"And that is the secret. I never let on how lost I was, because the minute I did everything else would have unraveled. I reckon my father felt this way as well. But he guided us, loved us, and I had to do the same. I wanted to do the same. So I went with my gut and sure, I made mistakes, but if people love you then they'll forgive you."

Heath stared at him. "Frankie loves you, Tom. She knows you're only human, but she looks to you to lead. She's a bit unsure, worried. She needs reassurance. I don't think Frankie has gotten over our parents' death. She probably thinks she has. Frankie internalizes everything. She doesn't like to talk about her feelings or her needs, as I'm sure you know. You have to coax them out of her. When she acts out, its often because she doesn't know how to talk about what is going on."

Tom knew that. And it was up to him to get her to talk. He thought they'd gotten past this. He realized now that he'd dropped the ball. That he hadn't seen how much trouble she was in.

"Do you remember what she was like before our parents died?" Heath asked.

Tom nodded. He remembered the girl who used to follow them around, constantly annoying them. "She was always getting into trouble."

"She was fearless." Heath grinned. "Always trying to catch up to her brothers. Mom used to despair that she had five boys, because Frankie was such a tomboy. And she adored my father more than all of us. He was her hero, and she was his little shadow. He spent far more time with her than any of us. I'm not saying that because I resent it, he gave us plenty of time and love, but Frankie was his darling.

"By the time she came along, the ranch was doing really well and he had the time free to spend with her. Frankie was open, happy, whatever she felt she'd be sure to tell you. After our parents died she became withdrawn. She pulled into herself. My point is that while she'll never be that same little girl again, it tears me up inside each time I see her worrying." Heath frowned. "I'm not trying to criticize you or anything."

Tom sighed. "It's okay. I can take it."

"She seems out of sorts and stressed."

"Yeah, I know. I think part of the problem is that soon after we got married, we started trying to have a baby. Each time she takes a test and it's negative, it just eats away at her a bit more."

Heath frowned slightly. "For all her bravado, she's quite sensitive."

"It was pointed out to me today that she thinks she needs to be perfect. To give me a perfect life." And he hated that Roarke had been the one to tell him that. Tom should have seen it. "How do I convince her that it is perfect because she's in it?"

"I'd start by telling her that. Can't be easy on her, with Bryony and Anna both pregnant," Heath continued. "Maybe what you both need is a complete break. Get away from everything for a while. Give her a chance to stop worrying so much and just be with you."

Tom closed his eyes for a moment, feeling exhausted. "I think you're right. I'll see if I can arrange some time away for both of us."

"You're welcome to go to the cabin, no one's using it and you'll be guaranteed privacy."

Tom opened his eyes and looked at Heath, grateful for his support. "Thanks, I think I'll take you up on that. Now, where is my wife?"

FRANKIE AWOKE as someone placed a kiss on her neck, moving down to her shoulder. She moaned softly and rolled sleepily onto her back to give those wandering lips more access. Warm lips pressed against hers, a tongue pressed into her mouth. She made a humming sound of pleasure. The lips disappeared and she came awake completely.

Sitting up suddenly, she slammed into Tom, crunching his nose with her forehead.

"Ouch," he protested.

"Oh God, Tom, I'm sorry," she said with concern, pulling his hand away from his nose to peer at it in concern. "Did I hurt you?"

"I'll live," he grumbled. Then he turned to her again, studying her. "I thought I left you with orders to rest?"

"I'm in bed," she pointed out.

He remained silent. Frankie shifted uncomfortably.

"Sorry," she said quietly. "I did text you."

"You did. And I should be the one to apologize for leaving like I did."

She sat up slowly and reached for his hand. "What's going on, Tom?"

Tom blew out a breath. "My past came back to haunt me."

"You went to see that guy? Who is he?"

"His name is Roarke Landon. And he's the man who killed my best friend."

Her heart raced, her mouth dry. "What? He's dangerous?"

He shook his head. "No. No, he'd never hurt you. You were as safe with him as any of your brothers, much as it might pain me to admit that." He let out a sigh. "I've told you about Austin, my best friend in college."

"The one who died when a drunk driver crashed into him?" He'd told her about Austin when they'd started dating.

"Yes. What I never told you is that Austin didn't die immediately. He lived on life support for several days."

"Oh God." She could see the pain on his face and it killed her.

"The reason he was out that night was because of an argument he'd had with his older brother, Roarke."

Tom looked across the room. It was clear he wasn't looking at the light-gray walls, but his mind was back on the past.

"Austin had fallen in love. Or he thought he had. Cara was a sub he met at a club Roarke owned."

She hadn't known that Austin had practiced BDSM.

"Austin used to drag me along to the club. It wasn't really my thing. I liked parts of it, but I wanted something more personal than essentially dominating a different sub each weekend." He looked at her. "I wanted what we have."

Her insides warmed.

"I didn't like Cara, but I respected his love for her. She was manipulative and catty. But he couldn't see it. Roarke could, though. They had a number of arguments over her. The last argument was the worst. Roarke told Austin that Cara was only with him to get to Roarke. That it was Roarke she wanted, not Austin, not a poor, young med student. Roarke has a lot of money. He's a powerful man, but he doesn't let people close. No one except family. He considered me family."

"What did Austin do?" she asked.

"He was furious. They both said things that were hateful. I was there. I watched as Austin stormed out of our small apartment and drove off. I didn't go after him. Didn't stop him."

She heard the regret and self-loathing in his voice.

"Tom, it wasn't your fault."

He turned to look at her, his eyes filled with so much pain that she sucked in a sharp breath. "Wasn't it? He was hit by a drunk driver. Roarke made the decision to turn off the life support. His parents couldn't do."

"Oh God, I'm so sorry." Frankie clasped him close, wishing she could take his pain into herself. "What about Roarke? He must have been devastated as well."

She couldn't even imagine his pain.

"He should be," her normally compassionate husband snarled. "He killed him."

"Tom—"

Tom stood, pulling away from her as he started to pace. "No, I don't want to hear any defense of him. He might as well have taken a gun to Austin's head and killed him."

She sucked in a breath. This was so unlike her husband. Couldn't he see how much Roarke must be hurting? That he'd only been trying to protect his brother? She might have done the same in a similar situation.

It seemed to her that the person to blame in this was the drunk driver. Not Roarke or Tom. Because she knew her husband blamed himself as well. And maybe that was why he was so angry at Roarke.

Tom turned back to her. "When I heard he'd opened that club in Waco I thought he might come see me. When he didn't, I was glad. I didn't want to see him."

"A BDSM club?" she asked.

Tom nodded sharply. "He has several."

"Is that how he knows Brax?" She knew her brother was in the lifestyle.

"Yeah, I guess so."

She licked her lips. She hated seeing Tom like this. Perhaps she could get in touch with Roarke, see if she could ease this rift. Maybe that's why he'd given her his card. He'd wanted Tom to see it. To get in touch. How hard could he be to find? Couldn't be that many people called Roarke who owned a BDSM club in Waco. Tom wouldn't be pleased at her interference, but she hated seeing him like this.

"I went and saw him. Warned him away from you. He won't be around for long, hopefully he'll soon head back to Austin."

So she'd have to move quickly.

6

They drove home in separate cars, giving her way too much time to think and worry. He hadn't said anything more about Austin or Roarke. She'd gotten up. They'd said a quick goodbye to her brother before driving home.

When she pulled up behind him, Tom walked over to open the door and help her out. She felt an impending sense of doom. She knew it was time to pay up and any more of a wait was going to kill her. She wished he'd gotten it over and done with this morning.

Moving inside, she went to the kitchen to get a glass of water. Tom leaned against the kitchen counter, watching her.

"What do you think about going away for a bit?" he asked suddenly.

She coughed as her mouthful of water went down wrong. He patted her back, taking the glass from her hand. "Okay, baby?"

"Yep. That wasn't what I was expecting you to say."

He grinned. "What? Were you expecting me to tell you to strip so I could bend you over the counter and spank you with the wooden spoon?"

She watched him suspiciously. "Are you going to do that?"

"Maybe." His eyes twinkled. He was way too happy over that thought.

She gave him a disgruntled look. He pulled her over so she stood between his spread legs as he leaned against the counter again. He kept his hands on her hips, holding her there.

"I think we could use some time away. Just the two of us. Heath has actually offered us the cabin."

"Can you get away?"

"It will take me probably a week to arrange cover, but yeah."

"Work may not give me time off." She bit at her lip.

"They should. You've got a lot of time owing and you've been working long hours covering shifts."

"I'll ask." She knew how he felt about her workload.

He ran his fingers through her hair. "I just don't like seeing you so stressed out. I have an idea about how to get you to really relax and let go. Our communication hasn't been the best lately and we need to get it back on track."

Hmm, she wasn't so sure about the sounds of that. Although getting a chance to relax and just be with him sounded amazing. "All right."

He leaned in and kissed her. "Now, we have something else to take care of. Go upstairs, strip, use the bathroom if you need to and then come back down and wait for me in the corner of the living room. Butt out, arms on your head."

Oh hell.

～

SHE WAS in no rush to go downstairs.

Tom had never required her to stand in the corner before a punishment. Afterwards, sure. Personally, she figured he just liked staring at her red butt, but she'd never had to wait for a punishment standing in the corner.

Knowing if she lingered much longer he would come looking for her, she left the bedroom and made her way downstairs. Putting this off wouldn't make it go away. And she really wanted the guilt eating away at her to disappear.

She moved to the only corner in the living room that didn't have a bit of furniture in it. Sticking her nose in the corner, she crossed her arms behind her back and widened her stance, sticking her bottom out.

She didn't know how long she stood there before Tom came into the room, but she'd nearly moved out of position several times. The embarrassment of this standing here combined with her trepidation was nearly too much for her to take.

"About time," she muttered quietly to herself, certain he couldn't hear her.

Smack!

"Ow," Frankie cried, jumping at the heavy spank that landed on her butt.

"Are you allowed to speak while standing in the corner like a naughty little girl?" Tom asked her.

God, those words, that tone of voice, it made her insides melt and she was flooded with the urge to submit.

"No, Sir," she replied softly.

"Then hush. I want you to stand right there. No moving. No talking. Understood?"

"Yes, Sir."

She closed her eyes, her throbbing butt cheek a reminder to behave. It was easier to stand here now, even knowing he was staring at her, because she had to do was what he told her to.

"Come here, baby girl."

Frankie turned, blinking herself out of her semi-trance. Tom sat on the sofa. She gulped as she saw what rested on the side table next to him.

"Tom?" she questioned, her gaze caught on the paddle.

He stared at her then down at the implements. He held up his hand. "A hand spanking for forgetting your dinner and hanging up on me." He then dropped his hand and picked up the paddle. "This is for not letting me know you were going out and putting yourself in a possibly dangerous situation."

Frankie gulped.

Tom patted his lap. "Lay yourself over my lap and we'll begin."

She shook her head. "I can't."

Tom simply stared at her. "Don't you want to get rid of that guilt rolling in your stomach?"

"Yes," she whispered. "But can't you just do it? Can't you just pull me over your lap?" Somehow it seemed much harder to have to do it herself.

"No, baby," he told her. "You can do this, Frankie. Give us what we both need."

Tears started rolling down her cheeks as she stepped forward and positioned herself over his lap. When she was settled, Tom rubbed her back.

"I'm very proud of you, Frankie," he crooned. "My brave, beautiful girl. Do you know how gorgeous you are when you submit to me? Remember it's not a sign of weakness. It's being strong enough to admit what you need and going after it. There are so many people who are too scared, but not my Frankie. This is going to be hard on you, honey. I can't go easy. I have to make an impression because I will not survive another night the way I spent last night. I want you to hold onto the sofa arm and don't move your arms. Understand?"

"Yes, Sir."

"Good. Then we'll begin."

His hand landed sharply, heavily. He moved swiftly, quickly covering the whole of her buttocks in smarting spanks.

Frankie dropped her head, tears forming as her butt burned.

Then throbbed. Each smack was loud in the quiet room. Her buttocks tensed in preparation of each strike.

Oh, God, would he never stop? She was all too aware of the rest of her punishment to come, but it seemed like Tom wasn't taking any of that into consideration. He was giving her one hell of a hand-spanking.

"I don't want you skipping any more meals," he told her, pausing briefly. "I don't tell you these things just to be controlling. It's for your health."

Pain engulfed her, radiating through her. She had to work hard to keep still when all she wanted to do was move out of the way of his punishing hand.

He stopped. "Will you be forgetting to eat again?"

"No, Sir." Sobs shook her, tears dripping down her cheeks. God, her ass was on fire. How could she take any more?

"Will you hang up or refuse to take my call?"

"No, Sir."

"Good, because this is a light spanking in comparison to what you'll get next time. I take your health and safety very seriously, Frankie."

"I-I know."

"We'll move onto the paddle. This part of your punishment is about safety. I never want to spend a night like I did last night, understand?"

"Yes, Sir."

"Good. I want you to count these out and ask me for the next. You have twenty."

Oh hell.

Smack!

The paddle landed, excruciating painful against her already roasted bottom. Tom stilled and Frankie caught her breath frantically. Oh crap. Oh hell. She out a shuddering breath.

"One. May I have another please, Sir?"

She cried out. Her ass was on fire. Each strike agony. Tom gently rubbed her bottom as he waited for her to count out the next one. As the paddle continued to land, she found herself almost drifting into the pain. It was still agony. She wouldn't be sitting comfortably for a while. But the pain also did something to her. It pushed away everything else. Fears. Worries. All gone as she just lay there and accepted her punishment.

By the time he reached twenty, Frankie was unable to count, her breath stolen by the punishing force of the paddle. Luckily, Tom sensed her problem and finished the count for her.

Huge, heartfelt sobs jumped out of her lungs as he turned her, holding her, careful not to let her bottom come into contact with his lap. She buried her face against his chest. This was the part she enjoyed about a punishment spanking, the cuddling afterwards when she felt so safe and protected within Tom's arms. When he took care of her.

He rubbed her back, crooning to her softly. She gradually stopped crying and just lay on his lap, exhausted.

"You did so well, baby. I'm proud of you."

His words warmed her. Made her feel loved.

"Do you want to have a lie-down while I make some dinner?"

She wanted to tell him that she'd just woken up, but then she yawned and realized how tired she was.

He lay her on the couch, on her stomach, and put a light throw over her. Then he leaned down and kissed her cheek.

"You make me so happy."

7

"Have you been to the bathroom?" Tom asked as he grabbed the suitcases to put them in the car. Frankie was busy running around checking all the appliances were turned off. Except the fridge. She'd made that mistake once before when they'd left on holiday.

She wouldn't make it again.

"I'm fine," she asked, only half-listening to him. After all, she was twenty-seven years old. She'd been going to the toilet by herself for years.

"I didn't ask if you were fine. I asked if you'd been to the bath-room," he said sternly.

Frankie gaped at him in shock. "Umm, yes."

"Good, go hop in the car, please," he said firmly.

She walked slowly to the car, wondering what she had really gotten herself in for. They'd both agreed that Tom was completely in charge for the next two weeks while at the cabin. Of everything. Frankie swallowed heavily. She'd agreed to this but could she really do it? Was she ready? But then, how did one even ready themselves for this?

By the time Tom walked into the garage she was a mess of nerves. She'd talked herself into this then out of it several times.

She was so involved in her thoughts that she barely noticed him climbing into the car until he reached across and took hold of her hand.

"Honey, stop worrying. For the next two weeks, I'm in charge. You don't have to worry about anything. You don't have to think, because frankly, you have no say in anything that goes on."

A shiver raced up her spine. "I don't get a safe word then?"

Tom raised his eyebrows. "And what do you know about safe words?"

She shrugged. "I've been looking them up."

"Have you just?" he murmured thoughtfully. She blushed a little. She'd been looking into Roarke's background. She'd managed to find the club he owned in Waco, but she hadn't worked up the courage to call him or go there. She wanted to help heal the rift between them. This was a man Tom had once looked up to and cared for. Frankie thought she might be able to help them both.

Frankie knew she'd be in a hell of a lot of trouble should Tom ever find out what she was contemplating, but this was hurting him and it was the least she could do for him when he did so much for her.

"If I ever do anything you don't like, tell me to stop and I will."

"Even when you're spanking me?" she asked.

Tom chuckled. "No, baby, that is one area where it won't work. I think this is what you need, don't you?"

"Maybe," she said, not wanting his arrogance to get out of control.

Tom just grinned and reached over to grab her seatbelt. "Let's get you buckled up and get on our way. We've got a bit of a drive ahead of us."

He did his own belt up before pressing the button for the automatic garage opener then reversing the car out.

"We're really doing this, then," she murmured half to herself.

"Yes, baby, we really are."

"Shit, I'm in trouble."

She yelped as Tom slapped her hand sharply. "No swearing. It wouldn't take much for me to pull this car over and put you over my knee."

Frankie's jaw dropped. "You wouldn't."

Tom remained quiet.

Damn it. The bastard would really do it.

Yep, definitely in trouble now.

FRANKIE FINISHED EATING. They'd stopped for lunch about two hours away from the cabin.

"Are you finished, honey?" Tom asked her. She nodded and pushed the plate away.

He stood, placing some money on the table for their bill. "Come on, bathroom break then we'll get on the road again. I know you must be getting tired. You're doing really well."

He held out a hand to her and she took it, letting him help her up. He kept hold of it as he turned and walked across the room to the bathroom.

"I don't need to be escorted to the bathroom," she told him.

"I didn't ask if you did."

With a huff to show she wasn't impressed, Frankie stomped into the bathroom, squealing as he gave her a sharp smack to her bottom on the way.

When she exited the bathroom he was standing there, waiting.

"Did you go?" she asked him sarcastically.

"Why yes, baby, I did. Come on, let's get going then. Thank

you," he called out to the waitress as they left. Frankie nodded and smiled, too embarrassed to say anything.

Tom settled her in the passenger seat, buckling up her seat-belt. But instead of immediately jumping into the driver's seat he took hold of her hands and kissed her forehead. "I love you so much."

"I love you too," she whispered back. Closing her door, he moved to the trunk of the car, rummaging around before climbing into the driver's side holding a pillow and a blanket.

"What are those for?" she asked suspiciously.

"It's time for you to have a little nap," he told her.

Frankie stared at him as he leaned down and pushed the lever on her seat, letting the back drop back. Frankie refused to lie down.

"No way, I'm not having a nap," she said stubbornly.

"You're run down, Frankie. You're pale and you've lost weight. I've been neglecting you and that stops now. Let's make you as comfy as possible so you can be all refreshed by the time we get to the cabin."

Frankie just gaped at him. "Frankie, I suggest you do as you're told," Tom told her in a low voice that promised punishment unless she did.

Shit.

"No," she told him, pushing the lever on her chair and the back of the seat rose up.

Tom just stared at her, then pushing the pillow and blanket into the back seat, he did up his seatbelt and started up the car. Frankie was surprised by how easily he'd given in, but hey, she wasn't going to question her luck.

She stifled a yawn as he pulled into a park. The parking lot was empty.

"Why are we stopping?" she asked. She had a bad feeling.

"We're stopping because someone needs a reminder about

obedience, and I didn't think the diner car park was the right place to spank you."

Her jaw dropped. Wow, he had never been this strict before. "You cannot be serious."

Ignoring her, Tom got out of the car, moving around to her side. Frankie watched him with an impending sense of doom. Everything seemed to slow down. Her door opened, he reached down and undid her belt, pulling her up. She didn't even fight him as he pulled her around to the backseat. Opening the door, he sat in and drew her across his lap.

Pushing him to see how far he would take this had not been a good idea.

Shit.

"Someone might see," she cried.

"Well, you should have thought of that before behaving like a brat," he told her calmly, lifting her skirt up to show her G-string.

Slam!

His hand landed with punishing force, immediately her skin stung, making her gasp. Frankie bit her lip, determined not to cry out. The last thing she wanted to do was draw attention to herself.

Smack!

Her other cheek was treated to the same stinging slap, his hand broad and heavy.

"When I tell you to do something, sweetheart, I expect you to do it."

Slap!

Damn it, she wished he would hurry up. She wanted this spanking over with. Now. But he seemed determined to take his time, scolding her between each searing spank.

"I know you're tired."

Smack!

She whimpered slightly. He might be going slowly, but his spanks were hard and left a burning pain in their wake.

Smack! Slap!

Two spanks landed in the middle of her ass, nearly covering both cheeks. She kicked her feet.

"I'm sorry," she cried out, hoping that might be the end of it.

"I'm sure you are." Smack! Smack! She wiggled, wanting free, but he held her tightly. "I'm sure you didn't think you'd be getting your bottom spanked out here where anyone could see." Smack! Smack!

"Please, sir, no more," she cried out, tears now tracking down her cheeks as he spanked her thighs slowly but steadily.

"Now you're going to have to ride the rest of the way on a sore bottom, aren't you?" Smack! Smack! "I bet you're going to be a very sorry little girl."

Frankie sobbed. Her ass was on fire and no, it was not going to be an enjoyable car ride. When he was done, he turned her over, tucking her against his chest as she cried. Gradually, she calmed, her bottom still stinging uncomfortably.

"There's a good girl. My beautiful girl."

He kissed the top of her head, before helping her off his lap to sit on the seat beside him. Frankie hissed as her bottom encountered the seat. She whimpered, the rest of the drive was going to be miserable. Tom reached down and grabbed the blanket and pillow. Exiting the back seat, he pulled her out behind him and opened her door. He helped her lie down, on her side, then drew the seat belt over her.

Placing the pillow under her head, he arranged the soft blanket over her before pressing a kiss to her head.

"Sleep well, honey."

"YAY! WE'RE ALMOST THERE."

Tom smiled at the excitement in Frankie's voice. Her nap, even though she'd resisted it, had certainly done her some good. She now had a sparkle in her eyes and some red flushing her cheeks. He'd worried he was pushing too far too fast, but had decided to take Heath's advice and go with his gut. Sure, it might be a mistake, but it was what he felt they needed.

Both of them.

He was going to push her comfort boundaries. He wanted to show her that she could trust him no matter what. That she could give him full control and that he would take care of her. He freely admitted that having her completely dependent on him was a turn on. Oh, he wouldn't want this permanently. He didn't want to be in charge all the time. But these two weeks were something he was looking forward to.

Somewhere along the way they'd gone off track. Stopped talking to each other. He was going to make certain that no longer happened. He wanted Frankie to know she could talk to him about anything. That she was everything to him.

Frankie bounced up and down then hissed. Obviously, her bottom was still smarting. Tom hid a smile. They'd stopped to buy groceries. There had been a few small arguments about what she wanted to eat and what he thought she should eat, although she'd been quickly subdued by his threat to pull up her skirt and spank her in the cereal aisle.

Frankie's hand drifted down to her buckle.

"Don't undo that belt until we've stopped," Tom warned her. She turned to look at him, obviously about to argue. He stared back at her sternly and she sighed, placing her hand back on her lap.

"I cannot wait to go for a swim."

"We'll go for a swim tomorrow," he told her as he brought the car to a stop. She had her belt undone and was out of the car almost before he could blink.

FRANKIE LOOKED around the guest bedroom. She was unpacking while he cooked dinner. She'd been coming here since she was a child. Her dad had built this cabin when Heath was just a baby. It had been added to over the years. There were two bedrooms in the cabin itself and a separate sleep-out with bunks. They were fairly isolated out here. The closest neighbors were about five miles away.

She'd had so many happy days here growing up. She wondered if she'd ever bring her own kids here? Sadness ran through her and she covered her stomach.

It could still happen. It would happen.

Desperately trying to shake off her feelings of melancholy, Frankie looked at the window again. This was the bedroom she always used when she came here. The boys took the sleep-out, although after their parent's death, Heath had stayed in the cabin with her. However, she'd often snuck out the window after her bedtime to tag along after her brothers.

They'd never told on her either.

Although she wondered if her parents had known. One morning her mother had asked her how the campfire went. The one her brothers had started around midnight the night before.

She grinned at the memory and quietly opened the window, climbing out. She headed off to the lake.

"FRANKIE, DINNER'S READY, HONEY," Tom called out down the passage.

No movement. No noise.

Tom frowned. "Come on, Frankie."

Still nothing.

With a shake of his head, he placed their plates on the counter and wiping his hands on a towel, walked down the passage to the bedroom. He opened the door.

To find the room empty and the window open. He rolled his eyes. He'd spent enough time at the cabin to know that Frankie used to sneak out the window to join her brothers. Everyone had known. Putting some shoes on, he grabbed both of their coats. Pulling his on, he trudged off towards the lake.

As he grew closer, he came to a stop, just watching her. She was so gorgeous. She was kicking water around, getting soaked and probably freezing to death. She wouldn't notice until someone pointed that out to her, though, then she'd start shaking. Her long, dark hair floated around her like a dark cloud, soft and shiny. He caught glimpses of her face—saw her wide grin.

Yes, coming here had the best idea for them both.

"Frankie," he called out softly.

She gasped, turning swiftly, her hand against her chest. "Tom, you scared me."

He crooked a finger at her, making sure the look on his face was stern. "Come here, now."

Frankie bit her lip, looking very cute as she dropped her gaze and walked toward him. She came to a stop before him. His heart sped up.

He placed two fingers under her chin. "Snuck out of the cabin, did you? And without telling me. Tut-tut."

She looked worried until he grinned down at her. "You know there's a perfectly good door, right? And that you should be wearing a jacket."

As soon as he mentioned it, she started shivering. He wrapped her jacket around her, then hugged her against him.

"I love you, baby. I'm glad we're here."

"Me too." She sighed and rested her forehead against his chest.

8

_____

She stepped out of the bathroom. It was strange to feel so uncertain when she'd been married to this man for close to year. But she was nervous. She knew that he intended to take complete control in the bedroom. As well as everywhere else. Part of her was filled with trepidation, but the rest of her was dying to experience what came next.

As she stepped into the bedroom, she found him lying on the bed. He was naked. All that silky, tanned skin on display. He was built like a runner. Slim but muscular. His abs rippled as he leaned back against the headboard. Her breath caught as he grabbed hold of his thick cock, running his hand up and down the shaft. He ran his thumb over the rounded head and her clit throbbed, her pussy already wet. Needy.

"Tom."

"It's Sir in the bedroom, sweetheart," he told her in a deep voice. "And you should be naked."

She looked down at the pale pink gown she was wearing.

"No more clothes for you in the bedroom. And if you're not

naked in the next ten seconds, then you will be spending all of tomorrow naked as well."

She'd never undressed so quickly in her life. She was actually panting a little by the time she'd pulled her panties off.

"Hmm." With one finger, he rubbed his chin. "New rule. No panties while we're on holiday."

Her eyes widened. "I can't do that."

"You can. You will. Or do you need a reminder of who is in charge?"

She shook her head frantically. "No, Sir."

He continued to run his hand up and down his shaft. His movements almost lazy, unhurried.

"Come here." He crooked a finger at her then held out his hand for hers as she reached the bed. "Climb on my lap."

She straddled his lap. He ran his hands up her thighs, making her shiver. Her pussy was pressed up against his cock. "Part the lips of your pussy," he told her. "I want to feel your slickness against my cock."

She blushed a little but lifted up a little then pushed the lips of her pussy apart. She moaned as her throbbing clit brushed up against his shaft.

"That's it. So wet for me. Good girl. Now, you're going to do exactly as I tell you, aren't you?" He ran his thumbs in small circles over her skin at the top of her thighs.

She shivered slightly. "Yes, Sir."

"That's what I like to hear. Reach up and grab hold of the headboard. Do not let go until I give permission. I want to suckle on those nipples."

Her heart racing so hard she almost felt dizzy, she was grateful for the support of the headboard as she did what he told her. Immediately he started to suckle on her right nipple. He held her hips, holding her steady, but otherwise all he did was suckle. Each pull of his lips against her tight nipple seemed to ripple down to her clit. It ached, longing for his mouth there.

She was panting for breath by the time he moved to the other nipple, so turned on and he'd barely even touched her.

"Please, Tom," she begged, wriggling her hips to get some friction against her swollen clit.

He pulled his mouth away from her nipple as he gave her a sharp smack on one buttock.

"What do you call me in the bedroom?"

"Sir," she whispered. "Sorry, Sir."

"Did I say you could move?"

She shook her head. "No, Sir."

"I am in charge of your pleasure. Not you. You do not come without my permission, understand? If I want to suckle on your nipples all night then I will. If I want to fuck you then tuck my cock inside your pussy while we sleep, without letting you to come then I will. And if I want to put a clit tickler on your clit then turn it on and off all night without allowing you release then I will do that."

"Holy shit," she whispered, his words lighting her insides until she swore she actually did come a little.

He leaned her forward, placing one arm over her back to hold her firmly while the other peppered her ass with sharp slap.

"Ow! Ow, Tom! Sir!"

"No swearing," he growled as he released her. "And you will remember how to address me."

The spanking hadn't really hurt. Sure, it stung a bit. But it had awakened other nerve endings. Her bottom was clenching, her clit on fire. God, she needed to come so bad.

But instead of rolling her over and taking her, Tom went back to suckling on her nipples. It was torture, having to lie still while he played with her nipples. The rest of her body was on fire with need. But somehow, she managed it.

And when he drew back, he looked up at her with a small smile. "Good girl.

"I'm going to help you off my lap sweetie, and then I want you on all fours on the bed, facing away from me."

He helped her off his lap. Slowly, she got down on all fours, facing the other way.

"That's my very good girl. I want you to split your legs wide. Wider."

Frankie parted her thighs so nothing was hidden from his sight.

"Now lower your chest down until its resting on the mattress." He waited until she had obeyed him. "Now I want you to reach back with both hands and part your bottom cheeks."

Tom watched as his wife reluctantly obeyed him. Her ass cheeks were a little red from that small spanking. Her puckered hole was revealed to him, stirring his blood. He knew he was pushing her. But they both needed this.

"Good girl. I'm very proud of you. I'm going to plug your bottom hole tonight." He ran his finger over her puckered entrance then pushed his finger slightly inside it. "I've neglected this area. I've never taken you here and that's a shame."

He hadn't taken her there because they'd been trying hard to get pregnant, something he intended to discuss with her. But not right now.

He moved over to the small bag he'd packed and put in the bottom of the wardrobe earlier. He drew out a plug and some lube and set them both down next to her face on the bed. She raised up, staring at him in shock. "That? That's huge. You can't put that in my ass."

"Turn around and bend back over, ass in the air," he told her sternly.

She stared at him in surprise.

"Now!" he barked.

She swiveled around, still kneeling, resting her face and chest on the mattress.

He smacked his hand down on her bottom in hard, stinging smacks. "You do not get to decide what I do to you. And you do not move out of position without permission, is that understood?"

He continued to spank her until she nodded.

"Words," he reminded her.

"Yes, Sir!"

He stopped and rubbed his hand over her red ass. Beautiful. "Good, any more disobedience and I will use the ginger lube." He slathered two of his fingers in lube then placed a small blob over her entrance. She gasped slightly.

"Breath in," he told her, pressing a finger over her hole. "Now out."

He pushed one finger deep inside her as she let her breath out. Damn watching his finger disappear into her asshole was a gorgeous sight. He moved up to two fingers, stretching her. Thrusting deep. Hot. Tight.

Tom ran the thumb from his free hand through her folds, feeling the moisture there. He flicked her clit as he drove his fingers in and out of her ass.

"Please, please. Tom, please," she begged, nearly breathless with arousal.

"Please what?" he asked.

"Please let me come."

"No," he told her.

She cried out. He barely held back his laugh. He withdrew his fingers then picked up the plug, covering it in lube.

"Right, breathe in again. This is going to be harder and I want you to stay relaxed."

"Do you know how hard it is to relax when someone is pushing a rod up your backside?"

He snorted. "No, I don't. But you're going to try your best. Right, let your breath out."

As she let out a shuddering breath, he pushed the plug slowly inside her. He had to push it past the tight ring of muscle and she let out a soft grunt. He stilled.

"All right, baby?"

"Yes, Sir."

Hmm, if he wasn't mistaken, she was growing even more turned on from having the plug pushed inside her. He reached around with his free hand and ran a finger through her folds. Yep. Nice and wet.

He pressed a finger deep inside her slick passage, moving the plug in tandem he drew his finger out. In then out. She shuddered, her cries filling the room.

"Please let me come, Sir," she cried out.

"Not yet."

"Nooo," she yelled out.

Again, he had to hide back a grin. Why hadn't he done anything like this before?

He seated the plug in her ass with a firm pat.

"Good girl, you're so beautiful, you know that, right?" The sight of her red butt, the butt plug between her cheeks, the wetness coating her folds and the top of her thighs almost had him coming before he even got inside her. He gritted his teeth as he knelt behind her and lined the head of his cock up against her pussy, pressing deep inside her. Her wet heat drew him in, surrounding him. It took all of his control not to come then and there.

"Oh honey, you have no idea how good that feels," he groaned. "You are so tight, so hot."

He pulled back then pushed forward.

"I feel so full," she cried.

"You're doing so well," he praised her, speeding up, thrusting his hips back and forth. Pleasure rushed over his body, making his legs tremble, his torso shake.

"I can't hold on much longer, sweetie," he warned her.

"I need to come. Please."

He reached around and flicked at her clit with his finger.

"Come for me, baby."

He felt the first tremors of her release and moved his finger faster, harder. She crashed over with a scream and he was gone. He drew back, drove forward and yelled aloud as he found his own shattering relief.

He managed to roll to his side so he wouldn't crush her. He pulled her up against his side, running his hand up and down her back. Sweat coated his skin, his heart was racing and he'd never felt better.

Leaning down, he kissed the top of her head. "Stay there, baby. I'll clean us both up."

He quickly washed himself off in the shower then grabbed a towel and ran some warm water over a cloth before moving into the bedroom. He found her just as he'd left her. She didn't even stir as he approached.

Hmm. He knew it was a little sneaky of him but in this state, it would be easier to get answers out of her.

He put the cloth and towel down and lay down beside her, running his thumb over her firm nipple.

"Honey?"

"Yes?"

"Do you think that you need to make everything perfect for me?"

She snuggled into him. "You deserve so much better than me."

He cupped her breast. "Why is that?"

She snorted softly. "Because you're amazing. You're talented, smart, gorgeous, patient and kind. And I'm just a fuck-up, I don't deserve you."

He had to force himself from growing tense and pulling her out of the semi-awake state she was in. But damn it, how could she think that?

"Baby, you are not a fuck-up."

"I'm not sweet and nice like Anna, or calm and together like Bryony. I feel like I'm always lost, as though I'll never measure up and be the wife you need."

"And what do you think will happen if things aren't perfect? If you aren't what I need?"

She was exactly what he needed. It made him feel ill to hear her speak like this.

"You'll leave me."

And that was the heart of it, he knew. She feared losing him. Didn't she know he felt the same way? He'd be devastated if he lost her.

"Honey, you'll never lose me."

"Can't guarantee it. Lost mom and dad."

He let out a shuddering breath. Heath was right. She hadn't truly gotten over her parents' death. And why would she? She'd lost two people who had loved and adored her. Who had been her world.

"Baby, I can't guarantee that nothing will happen to me. But I can tell you that I won't leave you because you're not perfect. That is not going to happen. I love you. I'm hardly perfect. I make mistakes. I do stupid things. I can be grumpy. I snore when I drink. I never remember to leave the toilet seat down and I get so caught up in my work sometimes that I don't give you the attention you deserve."

She stiffened and he knew she was more aware now. She sat, wincing a little. "The plug is still inside me."

"I'll take care of that in a minute," he told her, sitting next to her.

"Frankie, why didn't you tell me any of this? As soon as you started worrying about all of this, you should have come to me."

"In case you haven't noticed, I'm not really good at talking about my feelings and stuff." She gave him a narrow look. "Very sneaky, questioning me when my guard is down."

He reached out and took hold of her hand. "It got you to talk to me, didn't it? That's why we're here. To get things back on track. I'm sorry I didn't realize what was going on with you."

She shook her head. "No. This isn't your fault, Tom. It's all on me. I bottled it all up. You're right, I should have told you. I had this plan for our life together. I was going to try so hard to give you everything you wanted so you wouldn't see my faults. When nothing went the way I thought it would I didn't know how to handle it. My job wasn't as great as I thought it would be. I wasn't getting pregnant. I just felt like such a failure."

He pulled her close, hugging her tight. "You could never be a failure." He drew back so he could look into her face. "Baby, my life is already amazing. Do you know why? Because you are in it. You fulfil me. You are everything. Sure, you make mistakes, we all do. Me too. I know how much you want a baby. I do too. But even if we can't get pregnant, it will not make my life any less perfect. It just means we might have to come up with another plan. There's adoption, fostering, stealing a niece or nephew. Your brothers won't notice one missing."

She laughed.

"You know that life isn't actually perfect, right? But those imperfections they're actually what makes life worth living. A perfect life would be kind of boring, don't you think? Especially if it meant I didn't get to spank you." He grinned.

She snorted.

"I love you. You're never getting rid of me."

"I couldn't stand it if I lost you, Tom. It terrifies me.

"I would never leave you willingly. I love you. You are beautiful, kind, funny and you're the one I desire, the one I want to grow old with. You are stuck with me no matter what. Nothing is as important to me as you."

"What if you grow sick of my temper in a few years?"

Tom snorted. "Never. Frankie, I know who you are, I always have. Besides, I know just the cure for your temper."

He grinned as she rolled her eyes. He leaned in and kissed her. "You are an amazing wife. Whether we have a child or not does not change how wonderful you are. Sure, you do things sometimes that make me worry, that make me fear for your safety and I am always going to call you up on those. But that does not mean I love you any less. In fact, I think I love you a bit more every day."

She gave him a more convincing smile.

"I hate seeing you so stressed all the time. And I think part of it is your job. You're not happy, are you?"

She shook her head. "No."

"Please resign. You can find a new job. Or come work for me. Or stay at home. I don't mind what you choose, I just want you to be happy."

"I don't think working together would be a great idea."

"Maybe not. But we can work out something. Please?"

She nodded. "I'll think about it."

Relief filled him.

"I want us to make a pact, right now. If either of us feels lost or unsure or if we need something the other isn't giving us, we're going to ask. There is no judgment in our house, nothing we can't talk about. Promise?"

"I promise," she swore.

"Pinky swear."

She burst into laughter. "What?"

"Pinky swear." He held out his pinky to her.

"What are you? A twelve-year-old girl?"

His lips twitched as he tried to stare at her sternly. "Pinky swear," he said in a growly voice, dropping her onto the bed to tickle her. "Pinky swear."

"Okay, okay," she yelled. "I give in."

He sat back.

"Pinky swear," she told him.

9

"Come on," Frankie said impatiently. "Let's go."

She bounced on the balls of her feet as she waited for Tom to finish packing up the food for their picnic.

"Coming. Just let me grab a blanket and then I'll be there in a second," he called out.

Frankie was ready to go, dressed in her bright pink bikini. They'd been here a few days now and already Frankie felt happier, lighter. Of course, it was a bit of a learning curve, giving over all her control to Tom, but once she'd stopped fighting herself, she'd found it freeing.

And it made her feel closer to Tom. As though he now knew all of her, and he hadn't run. It was a revelation.

"Right, all set." He walked out carrying the picnic basket, a blanket and two towels resting on the top of it. He was dressed in swimming shorts and a t-shirt.

"Yay!" Frankie opened the door and bounced outside.

"Excited, honey?"

"I love the lake and swimming."

"I know you do." He smiled at her as they walked along. He held her smaller hand in his protectively.

"Want me to carry something?" she asked.

"No. You don't carry your own bags when I'm around."

"Tom?"

"Yes, baby?"

She gave him a shy smile. "I really enjoy being here with you, like this."

Tom smiled, his eyes filled with happiness. "Me too."

"Sometimes I wish we could stay here forever," she said wistfully.

Tom raised his brows. "You want this arrangement permanently?" he asked, his surprise evident.

"Oh no." She shook her head. "I think I'd kill you eventually. I like having you in charge, I feel closer to you. I trusted you before but now it's been taken to a higher level. But I will eventually want to make some of my own decisions. No, I just meant being together, the two of us. It's nice."

"Yes, honey, it is. How about we make a promise to each other that we'll get away together up here at least three times a year?"

Frankie beamed up at him. "I'd like that."

He squeezed her hand. "Then that's what we'll do."

Frankie squealed as they got close to the water. She pulled at Tom's hold on her, wanting to run ahead, but he held onto her tightly.

"Hey, what's the rush," he teased. "The lake will still be there in two minutes."

"Urgh, you're such a spoilsport sometimes," she groaned.

He chuckled then let go of her hand. "Off you go, then," he told her with a heavy slap to her ass.

Frankie poked her tongue out at him, before taking off with a squeal. Tom dropped his stuff and took off after her.

"Ooh, you're in trouble when I get you," he yelled.

Frankie just laughed.

"Right, baby, let's get out. I'm hungry," Tom told Frankie as they played in the water.

"I'll be in soon, okay?"

"All right. Don't take too long. I don't want you getting too tired."

"Can't have that." She winked. Their sex life had been off the charts since they'd arrived at the cabin

He grinned. "No, you'll need some energy for later." Squeezing her butt cheek, Tom turned and swam lazily back to shore.

God, he was so lucky. Frankie was amazing, beautiful, sensual and dynamic, plus she had this other side to her that was vulnerable, open and childlike. He adored the whole package that made up his wife.

Coming here a few times a year would be good for them. Give them both a chance to relax and rejuvenate and to indulge in whatever sort of play they felt like.

Tom dried himself off and put his t-shirt back on before laying out the blanket and pulling the picnic basket over. When it was unpacked to his satisfaction, he looked out at the lake.

"Frankie, time to come in," he called out, frowning when he couldn't see her straight away.

Then he saw her out in the distance. A lot further out than she'd been before.

He stormed to the edge of the water, fighting back his fear. Frankie was a strong swimmer, she'd probably just lost track of how far out she was.

"Frankie!" he yelled louder. "Get back here now!"

Her head bobbed as she looked back at him. He breathed a

sigh of relief as she started back. Tom's worry grew at how slowly she was moving.

If she was dawdling out of defiance he was going to make sure she couldn't sit down for the rest of their holiday.

He tore off his t-shirt, and strode into the water, determined to go and get her. His heart literally stopped as Frankie raised her hand into the air, showing him her closed fist. It was their signal if one of them was ever in trouble in the water.

Tom raced through the water until it got to waist level, then he struck out, swimming steadily towards her. Getting closer, he saw she was just lying on her back, floating.

"Frankie," he called out as he got closer. He wrapped his arm around her, helping support her. "What's wrong?"

She smiled at him weakly. "Sorry, I didn't know I was so far out and I was getting so tired. I was scared to keep going so I decided to float for a while."

Panic threatened to overwhelm him at the weakness in her voice, her pale skin. He squashed the feeling. He was a doctor; he'd dealt with emergency situations before.

But never one with his own wife.

"It's okay, honey, you did the right thing. I'm going to pull you into the shore, all right? Then we'll get you all warmed up."

He began to swim with one arm, kicking his feet steadily.

"I'll help," she said quietly.

"No," he said sharply as he saw her legs start to move. "You just lie there."

"Okay." Her voice wobbled a little and he instantly felt terrible.

"I'm sorry, baby. I shouldn't have spoken so harshly. It's all right. You just really scared me."

Tom reached the shore eventually and standing, pulled her up into his arms. Carrying her over to the blanket, he got her towel and quickly dried her. Then he haphazardly chucked the food into the basket before wrapping her up in the blanket. Her teeth chattered, her skin pale and cold as he held her on his lap and took her pulse.

It was slow.

"I'm sorry," she said pitifully, her eyes filling with tears. "I'm sorry."

"Shh, baby," he told her, kissing her forehead. "It's all right. I'm going to get you back to the cabin and warmed up then I'll make you a hot chocolate, all right?"

She nodded.

Tom packed up the rest of their stuff and placed the handles of the basket over one arm. He glanced down at her, worried at her pale listlessness as she lay there, her eyes closed. She must have gotten a hell of a scare, he knew he had.

"Okay, sweetheart, let's get you back to the cabin." Crouching, he picked her up in his arms.

Frankie gasped, her eyes opening. "I can walk."

He snorted. "Like hell, honey, you can barely keep your eyes open. Now, stop fussing and just lie quietly like a good girl."

"Okay," she agreed, making him worry even more, it wasn't like Frankie not to argue a point.

FRANKIE OPENED her eyes as she heard Tom enter the room. He placed a steaming mug of hot chocolate on the bedside table then sat beside her, placing his doctor's bag on the floor beside him.

After carrying her all the way home, he'd put them both in a hot shower, the cabin didn't have a bath, and supported her as he warmed them both up. Then he'd dried her off, and placing her in some fleecy pajamas, put her to bed. Frankie hadn't even bothered to protest that it was only two in the afternoon. She was exhausted.

Tom grabbed her wrist and turned it over, holding two fingers over her pulse while he stared at his wristwatch. He then reached into his black bag and grabbed his stethoscope. She loved watching him in doctor mode. Pulling back the covers slightly, he undid the buttons on the front of her pajama top and pulling the sides apart, placed the rounded end of the stethoscope on her chest.

"I'm not sick, Tom," she said gently.

He just stared at her sternly. "Take a deep breath in. Now out."

With a soft sigh, Frankie did as she was told, letting him help her sit so he could check the back of her chest.

Tom helped her lie down. "Roll over. I want to take your temperature."

"But Tom, I'm fine," she whined, starting to feel a bit more alert. For a while there she'd felt as though she was outside her own body, almost drugged.

Tom frowned. "I don't like your color and your pulse is sluggish. I will be taking your temperature, whether I do it now or after a spanking is up to you."

"You know that they have these thermometers nowadays that take your temperature orally?"

He just gave her a look, unimpressed.

Frankie rolled with a grumble. Tom lowered her pajama pants. He hadn't bothered putting any panties on her. He parted her butt cheeks with one hand as she blushed deeply. She groaned as she felt the thermometer press against her puckered entrance.

"Relax baby, while I put the thermometer in."

Frankie squirmed until Tom slapped one of her buttocks in warning. She stilled and he slipped the thermometer inside her ass. Burying her head in the pillow, Frankie tried to pretend she was anywhere else until he pulled it out again.

"Temp's a little high."

Tom pulled her pajama pants up and rolled her again, helping her sit up. He even fluffed the pillows behind her so she was comfortably supported.

"Drink your hot chocolate, love. I want you to stay in bed for the rest of the day." He ran his hand over her hair. "Are you sure you're okay, Frankie? You're very quiet."

Frankie chewed at her lower lip as she glanced away from him. She worried the blanket covering her with her fingers.

"Frankie?"

"I guess I just got a bit scared is all. I didn't realize how far out I was and then I was so tired, I couldn't keep going, I just..." she trailed off with a sob, tears filling her eyes.

Tom gathered her close, holding her on his lap and rocking her. "Shh, baby, it's okay. I understand. You scared ten years off my life, that's for sure."

She hugged him tight, realizing this is what she'd been needing. To feel Tom holding her, surrounding her with his safety.

Tom pulled her back so he could look down into her face. "Please don't ever scare me like that again, Frankie. I couldn't stand it. You mean the world to me. I don't ever want to experience that sort of terror again." She could see he meant every word. He really did love her. Oh, she'd known he had. But now she could see that he was just as scared of losing her as she was of losing him. Her insides warmed.

"I won't. I promise. I love you."

"Love you too, baby."

10

L ooking up, Frankie smiled as Tom placed a glass of water beside her on the coffee table before sitting next to her to read his book.

They'd been at the cabin for eight days now and Frankie was thriving under the care and attention Tom lavished on her. This time together was special and something she'd never forget. Tom had truly shown her how much he loved her over this last week. And Frankie felt closer to him than ever. When they got home, she was going to make a real effort to communicate better with him.

She'd been unable to hide anything from him these last few days, he hadn't allowed that. But rather than feeling vulnerable or exposed, Tom had made her feel safe, secure.

She sighed. "I wish it wasn't raining." It was miserable outside and showed no signs of letting up.

Tom put his book down. "What can we find you to do that will keep you out of mischief, hmm?"

"Well, I can think of something," she suggested rubbing her hand down his arm.

"Can you just?" Leaning in, he kissed her, his hand

coming up to cup her breast. Frankie whimpered as he brushed his thumb over her nipple. It instantly pebbled beneath his touch as a shot of pure pleasure raced straight down to her pussy.

Unable to bear the clothes between them, Frankie climbed off his lap and hastily stripped. Once she was naked, she looked over to see Tom had shed his clothes and was sitting on the sofa.

"Kneel," he told her.

Frankie dropped gracefully to her knees and spread her legs wide as he'd taught her, keeping her back straight. He'd taken complete control everywhere, but this was where she truly enjoyed being dominated. And she didn't want it to stop once they left the cabin.

He'd reassured her that he didn't want to take her to a club, that he didn't want to take her anywhere where someone might see her. But in the bedroom, she was all his. And she loved it.

Her breath came in short, hard bursts as she stared over at him, drinking in the handsome man that was her husband. He grew more attractive with each year that passed. Her gaze roamed over his flat stomach down to his cock, standing firm and hard. She licked her lips.

Tom groaned. "God, baby, the things you do to me when you look at me like that."

"Like what?" she asked.

"Like I'm your favorite treat and you can't wait to eat me up," he told her, his eyes dark with arousal.

"Hmm, what a good idea. May I, Sir?" she asked.

Tom parted his legs wide, his eye lids at half-mast as he gazed at her.

"You may."

She shuffled forward, kneeling between his open legs. Leaning forward, she licked her way up his long, thick cock.

Tom took a quick breath. "That feels so good, baby. So good.

Here." He handed her a cushion for her knees, she sent him a smile of thanks, warming at his caring.

Clasping her hand around the base of his shaft, she sucked the head of his shaft into her mouth, flicking her tongue over the underside. She felt him shudder and smiled, glad she could do this for him. Wasn't like she didn't love doing it.

"That feels so good. You have no idea what you do to me. I am not going to last like this, honey."

Frankie slowly took him inside her mouth, then moved fast back up. Slow down, fast up. She heard him groan as she squeezed the base of his shaft.

"Baby, you're too good at that. Enough." Reaching down, he pulled her off him. Frankie made a grumbling noise. She wanted him to come in her mouth. "No more. I want to come in your sweet pussy, not your mouth. Behave." His stern voice had her quieting her protest.

Standing, he drew her up, swinging her into his arms so she was cradled against his chest. Frankie gasped.

"Tom, be careful of your back."

He glanced down at her incredulously. "Honey, you don't weigh a thing."

It was Frankie's turn to give him a look of disbelief. She was just shy of five-foot-eight and curvy with it.

They quickly reached the bedroom and Tom threw her lightly onto the bed. Frankie sat, but he pushed her back gently.

"Lie still," he ordered. "Arms above your head."

Her heart pounding, she did as he ordered.

"No moving, Frankie," he warned her before turning away to the wardrobe. His bag of tricks. When he turned back, Frankie's breath was coming in short bursts. He held some silk scarves and a face mask.

"You okay, baby?" Tom asked as he settled beside her and started attaching her wrists to the wrought iron headboard.

"Yes, Sir," she replied as he moved on to her feet, doing the same until she was spread-eagled, open and at his mercy.

"Remember, baby, you tell me to stop and I will."

"I won't want to stop!" She was already on fire with her need for him. He settled the eye mask over her face. An instant feeling of submissiveness fell over her. She loved the mask. It heightened everything else. Not knowing what was coming just made it that much more exciting.

She thrust her hips up suggestively. She wanted his touch on her pussy, her clit. Craved it. He half rolled her, smacking his hand down sharply on her butt cheek.

"Ow," she complained.

"Hold still or I'll take my paddle to your butt," he warned. Frankie immediately stilled.

"Are you wet for me, baby?" he asked in a deep voice as he ran a finger down between her breasts. He leaned in and licked one nipple then the other. He sucked one into the warmth of his mouth as he lightly pinched the other between his fingers.

"Frankie, answer me."

There was a warning in his voice she knew better than to ignore. If she wanted to come tonight that was.

"Yes. Yes, I am. Please touch me there, Sir. I can't stand it."

"Shh, yes you can. And remember, there's no coming without my permission. Or I'll get the belt."

She hated the belt. He moved down her body, swirling his tongue over her stomach. Oh God. Oh God. He hadn't even touched her clit and already she felt close to exploding.

"Please, oh please," she cried.

"Ahh, I love it when you beg. Not yet, though, I'm not finished playing. Spread your legs nice and wide."

He ran a finger through her folds, moving it lightly over her clit.

"Oh, it burns. Please, more."

"More?" He chuckled. "More what?"

"Touch my clit. Flick it. Make me come. Please."

She felt the weight on the bed shift. Where was he going? She pushed away the slight panic. Tom wouldn't leave her. She heard a buzzing noise before she felt him return. And then she felt a vibration against her clit. Frankie yelled, trying desperately to hold back her orgasm, but it slammed into her, bursting over her in flashes of fire.

"Oh God, oh God, I'm sorry," she cried after the waves of pleasure had worked their way through her body.

Being tied up, without her sight had only added to her sensitivity, making it impossible for her to hold back her pleasure.

Tom clicked his tongue and pulled off her eye mask. His face was stern, but she caught a glimpse of pleasure in his hazel-colored eyes. "You'll have to be punished for that. I didn't give you permission to come, did I?"

"No," she groaned as he grabbed hold of her legs, holding them up against her chest with one hand as he smacked her ass with his other hand. Frankie cried out as her bottom stung with each smack.

"Goddamn it, I should torture you until you're begging me to let you come, but I just can't hold on," Tom groaned as he knelt before her, swinging her legs over his shoulders. Grabbing hold of his cock, he leaned down on one hand and started to push his cock into her pussy. He stretched her, pressing into her. Her pussy clenched down, nerve endings dancing as he entered her.

"Yes, oh yes," Frankie groaned, her head thrashing back and forth on the pillow. "More, more."

He moved slowly. Too slowly. Inch by agonizing inch. Didn't he know what he was doing to her. Once he was fully inside her, he placed his thumb against her clit, flicking it. Slow then fast then slow. She whimpered. Orgasm built in the base of her spine and she knew it wouldn't take much for her to explode.

He drew back. Thrust forward. Filled her over and over. Until she could barely breathe, until she couldn't speak, couldn't even see.

"Come with me, baby. Come on, come with me now."

Wave after wave of excruciating bliss overtook her. She barely heard his own shout of satisfaction as he came inside her.

Shaking, small trembles of release still rocking her, Frankie gasped for breath. "Wow. Just wow."

"Amen to that, baby," he agreed.

11

Tom was going to kill her. Frankie knew it. Her butt was toast when he heard about this. But she'd started on this path and she wasn't going to turn back now.

No way.

Even if he roasted her ass every night for a week, it was going to be worth it if she could help fix things between him and Roarke. She took a deep breath. She was doing the right thing. Maybe. Nerves almost had her running the other way. But she was made of tougher stuff than that. Besides, she was doing this for Tom, to try and heal the rift between him and Roarke. This anger he was holding on to wasn't healthy. They'd been back a week and she'd decided after some more encouragement from Tom to hand in her notice. Her boss had tried to promise her all sorts of things to keep her on, but it was time for a change.

She and Tom were closer than ever. She'd never been happier. There was only one thing she couldn't get past. This rift between him and Roarke. So tonight, she'd come to Indulgence in the hopes that Roarke was still here. That she could do something to fix things between them. It was open night at the club, so she knew that she'd at least get through the door.

She hoped, anyway.

At least Brax wouldn't be here tonight. That would be awkward. Tonight was for people curious about the lifestyle, who wanted to test the waters, ask questions, and maybe play a little. Or so the website stated.

Slowly, she walked up the steps to the entrance and pressed on the doorbell. The door opened so suddenly she gasped. A large man stood in the doorway, his head waxed, tattoos covering his dark arms. She nearly turned tail and ran.

He raised a dark brow. "You coming in, kitten?"

"Y-yes?"

"Now, you don't sound too sure about that," he drawled.

Frankie straightened her shoulders. *I can do this.*

"I'm coming."

"Well, not yet, but maybe by the end of the night you will be." He winked at her and she blushed bright red.

"Oh no ... I'm not ... I mean ... I'm married," she blurted out.

His face grew stern. "Then where is your husband, kitten? He let you come here without him?"

"No," she replied hotly, bristling at the hint of derision in his voice. "He doesn't know where I am."

"That so? You're a brat, then. Well, I hope he spanks you good when he finds out."

"Oh, don't worry, he will," she muttered.

The man chuckled. "I like you, kitten. You'd be a handful to be sure, but I've always liked my subs with a bit of a challenge in them. Come inside then."

"Thanks." She followed him in. "Umm, I'm Frankie." He took her lightweight coat. He stared down at her in admiration. She tugged at the high hem of her red dress. Maybe she should have worn something a little less tight, a little less revealing.

"Stop playing with your dress," he barked. She immediately stopped, although she frowned at him.

"It's rude to just snap at people like that," she told him primly. "What's your name?"

"I'm Joe. Keep up that attitude and I might just decide to play with you a bit tonight."

She gaped at him. "No, uhh, I'm not here to play. Married, remember?" She held up her ring finger.

"So why are you here, kitten?" he asked.

"Don't you have other people to look after? It's awfully quiet, isn't it?" She looked around the empty foyer. She guessed everyone was out the back. Maybe this place wasn't very popular.

"Everyone else arrived on time, kitten. Only you were late."

"Oh." She bit her lip. "I got a bit nervous. I didn't think it would matter, being late."

"It matters. In fact, Master B might decide to take his displeasure over your tardiness out on your butt."

She gasped, feeling a bit ill at the thought of someone other than Tom touching her.

"Now, I'd like an answer to my question. I don't like to be kept waiting either."

Jesus, this man flicked from cheerful and teasing to stern at the flicker of an eyelid. What the hell had he asked her?

"Roarke," she bit out. "I'm here to see Roarke."

Instantly Joe shut down. "If that's all you're here for, sweetheart, then I'm afraid you're destined to be disappointed. Roarke doesn't play with newbies."

"No, I mean, I don't want to play with him, I just want to talk to him. He'll see me, I know he will. Please, just ask."

His gaze softened. "All right, kitten. Come on, I'll introduce you to Master B. I'll ask Roarke, but don't be surprised if he doesn't see you."

"He will, I know. Can you please tell him Frankie's here?"

ROARKE STARED DISINTERESTEDLY out of the large window of his office into the playroom below. His office was on a mezzanine floor, completely hidden from view by tinted one-way windows. Newbie night. He used to enjoy it. Used to participate, take an interest in their enthusiasm, their shock.

"You're not going down there? You used to like newbie night."

He glanced over at Sam, his friend, his lover, his submissive. Sam was the one thing in Roarke's life he knew he could count on. Oh, he had his family, but they didn't understand him, and after Austin's death he'd distanced himself from them. He knew that had hurt them, but sticking around would have hurt them more.

He shrugged. "Been to one, been to them all."

Currently the group were all before the St Andrews Cross watching as two of his team, Jax and his sub Olympia, demonstrated its use.

"We could go and demonstrate some of the equipment," Sam said, a hint of frustration in his voice.

Roarke turned to look at him, frowning slightly. "Are you feeling neglected?" He hadn't played with Sam for a while.

Sam shrugged, dropping his eyes. "You've had other things on your mind."

Roarke silently cursed himself. Yeah, he'd had things on his mind. Tom. Austin. But none of that excused neglecting Sam. He might be successful, rich, powerful, but the only happiness in his life came from Sam, the one person he could not live without.

Come here," Roarke said deeply. "Strip and kneel before me."

Sam's eyes lit up.

Damn, I have been acting like a real ass. Neglecting Sam was unforgivable.

Standing, Sam reached for the bottom of his t-shirt when

someone knocked on the door. Sam stilled, but Roarke gave him a stern look.

"Sam," he warned.

The other man continued to strip, after giving Roarke a cheeky grin. Damn sub.

"Come in," Roarke snarled. "And it had better be good."

By this time, Sam's magnificent chest was bare. Tanned, muscular and wide. Roarke didn't move his gaze from Sam's body as Joe entered.

"Roarke, sorry to interrupt," Joe said apologetically. He looked over at Sam. "Very sorry."

By now Sam was down to his underwear, his cock firm, pressing against his boxer shorts.

"What is it?" Roarke asked, holding his hand up to still Sam. He was hellishly possessive and even though he and Sam played plenty in public, he didn't often demand that Sam get completely naked. He pointed at his feet. Sam walked over and knelt, his movements graceful.

"There's a woman here, says she knows you. Cute thing. Mouth on her, though. Just added her to the group. Reckon Brax will take her in hand."

"Joe," Roarke said sharply, wanting the other man to get to the point. Quickly. He needed Sam's talented mouth around his dick, sucking him deep. Joe was a great guy, but damn, he could talk.

"She wants to speak to you."

"No," Roarke replied.

"That's what I figured," Joe said amicably, showing no offense at Roarke's short reply. "I'll go tell Frankie she's out of luck."

Frankie?

"Wait." Roarke stood as Joe turned to go. "What's her name?"

"Frankie. Not a very feminine name for a woman with all those curves."

"She's about five-foot-eight, dark hair, deep brown eyes?" Roarke asked urgently.

"Yeah, you know her?" Joe asked with interest.

Roarke might be bisexual, but he hadn't shown an interest in women since meeting Sam. People who didn't know him well thought he was gay. But he and Sam had often talked about adding a woman as their third. Not that he was interested in Frankie like that, she was off limits.

"Wait, she's in the playroom?" Fuck, Tom would murder him. "With Brax?" He pushed past Joe who was gaping at him. He heard both men following behind him, but didn't spare them a backward glance as he raced down the stairs.

The stairs exited into a changing room, the playroom was beyond. He didn't have to go that far, however. Brax and Frankie stood in the otherwise empty changing room, Brax looming over her sister, his face red with fury.

"What the hell are you doing here, Frankie?" Brax yelled, his hands firmly around his sister's shoulders as he shook her. Roarke bristled, surprised by his protectiveness towards the vixen who was glaring up at her older brother.

"What am *I* doing here? What are *you* doing here? This is newbie night. You're not supposed to be here."

Roarke watched on in silence, feeling Joe and Sam step up behind him. The fighting siblings hadn't seen them yet and he thought he might get his answers quicker by waiting and watching.

"What are you talking about? How did you even know about this place? What do you mean I'm not supposed to be here because its newbie night?"

"Well, I figured you wouldn't be here because you're not exactly new to BDSM."

The duh was very clear in her voice and Roarke felt his lips twitch. He heard Sam snort behind him. Joe was worse, he chuckled.

Brax looked over at them, frowning. He straightened as he saw who it was. "Sorry, Roarke, I, ahh, need to leave early I'm afraid. I need to deal with a family matter."

Brax grabbed hold of Frankie's upper arm and attempted to drag her from the room. He managed a few steps until Frankie grabbed hold of one of the pillars and held on for dear life.

"I am not going home with you, Brax."

"Let go of that pole, Frankie, or I'm gonna turn you over my knee right here and blister your butt."

Frankie went bright red, her eyes shooting daggers at Brax. Roarke did grin this time. Damn he hadn't been this amused in, well, years.

"You can't spank me, Brax Jamieson. Tom will kill you."

"Tom will thank me before he spanks you for coming here. Does he have any idea where you are?" Brax asked her.

She lowered her gaze guiltily. Which was what Roarke had expected, no way would Tom let her come here, certainly not alone.

"You are in so much trouble, little sister," Brax told her. "Now, let go of the pole so I can get you home to face your husband."

Frankie stubbornly shook her head.

Joe chuckled behind him. "She's a firecracker. Damn, it would be fun to tame her."

Both Roarke and Brax glared at him. He held up his hands in supplication. "Just saying."

Frankie grinned. "You couldn't handle me," she said cheekily.

Joe laughed. "Probably right there, kitten."

Roarke scowled at him.

"You know what," Joe said quickly. "I think I should get into the playroom, what with Brax out here they'll be a bit short-staffed." He fled the room.

Roarke looked over at Frankie and Brax. Brax was looking flushed. A combination of anger and embarrassment, Roarke guessed.

"Why don't you come up to my office, we'll talk there," he said. He wanted to know why Frankie would risk her husband's ire to come here.

Frankie nodded and looked up at Brax who reluctantly let her go with a glare. Frankie snorted and calmly walked up to Roarke, who held out his arm to her. She slipped her little hand into the crook of his elbow.

"Thank you, Roarke. Nice to know there are still some gentlemen around."

Brax made an irritated noise as he followed behind.

Roarke smiled down at her. "You're in a lot of trouble."

She sighed. "I know, but I had to talk to you."

"All right, let's go and talk."

He started up the stairs, Frankie beside him.

"Roarke, can I ask you a question?" she asked sweet as pie now that she was getting her way. Oh yes, she was definitely trouble.

"You may," he granted, expecting she'd ask him something about the club or his relationship with Tom.

"Why is there a man dressed just in boxers following you around?"

Roarke let out a bark of laughter.

FRANKIE TRIED to keep her gaze off the muscular chest of the man sitting across from her. Sam. Roarke's lover and submissive, he'd explained. Fancy that. She hadn't realized Roarke was gay.

"Sam, perhaps you'd best get dressed. I don't think Frankie's going to be able to concentrate otherwise," Roarke said dryly.

Frankie flushed as she realized she'd been staring. "I'm sorry. It's just, well, you're magnificent," she said to Sam who grinned.

"Frankie!" Brax barked. "You've got a husband at home."

She glared over at her brother. She couldn't believe her bad luck. What the hell was Brax doing here tonight? "I'm not blind. I can notice when another man is hot." She crossed her arms over her chest.

"What did you want to see me about, little one?" Roarke asked.

"Oh, well, it's kind of private. Can we speak alone?"

Roarke stared at her, Frankie squirmed, feeling like he could see her insides, her every thought. Damn, the man had her wanting to blurt out every bad thing she'd ever done.

"Sam knows everything about me, sweetheart. And I don't think that Brax is going to leave you."

"Damn straight," Brax agreed, his own arms crossed over his chest, his stare mulish.

"Brax," she sighed. "Please leave me alone for a bit. I won't go anywhere, I promise."

Her brother stared at her.

"I'll have Sam come find you when we're finished," Roarke added. "I won't leave her side."

Brax looked between them. "Fine." He stood and glared at her, pointing his finger at her as though she were a naughty two-year-old. "Stay put. Do as Roarke says."

Frankie congratulated herself on her control. She didn't stick her tongue out at him until he'd turned his back. "I saw that," he called back before opening the door and leaving.

She looked over at Roarke and Sam, who had to be the most gorgeous man she'd ever seen with his white-blond hair and startling blue eyes.

"If you've finished staring at Sam, honey, maybe we should talk," Roarke said, his voice amused.

"Oh, yes, sorry," she said to Sam again. He winked at her.

"I'm surprised you're here, little girl, I felt sure Tom would have ordered you to stay away from me, he certainly warned me away from having contact with you. Unless you're truly here for newbie night?"

Frankie waved that away. "No, I came to see you. I thought this might be the easiest way. Tom told me never to talk to you, never to see you, blah, blah, blah. He doesn't know I'm here, and really, he doesn't need to." Her butt would feel a lot better if he never found out. She wondered how she could bribe Brax to keep quiet.

Roarke raised an eyebrow. "I think that dream flew out the window when Brax saw you here. Not terribly obedient, are you? Perhaps Tom needs to spank you harder."

"Tom spanks me just fine," she snapped back at the implied criticism. She flushed as she realized what she'd said. "Look, I didn't come here to talk about me. I came here to talk about Tom. And you. I want to try to help the two of you fix this rift."

"Do you just?" Roarke's voice grew icy and Frankie nearly turned tail and ran. But Sam smiled at her and gave her an encouraging nod.

Frankie took a deep breath. "I don't understand why Tom is so angry with you. It's not healthy, for either of you. Tom once thought of you as family. He's letting his pain and his own guilt blind him and he's blaming you for something that wasn't your fault. That's not fair."

Roarke was silent for a long moment and she thought he was going to refuse to talk to her. "But it was my fault. I killed Austin."

Frankie shook her head, leaning forward. "No, you didn't. A drunk driver killed Austin. It wasn't your fault."

"If I hadn't had that fight with him, he would never have been out on his bike that night. He would still be alive. Tom's entitled to his anger. I suggest you leave him to it. It was completely my fault and my punishment is to have to live every day knowing I lost my brother and my family."

"Your family?" she asked, shocked. What had happened to his family?

"They blame me."

"They said that?" Jesus, what had this man lived through?

He shook his head, his gaze locked over her shoulder. "No, but how could they not? I don't believe this has anything to do with you, Frankie. Perhaps it's time you left."

Sam urged her on silently, his eyes pleading with her not to give up.

"It wasn't your fault, Roarke. And I think the person blaming you the most is yourself."

He raised his eyebrows, his gaze sardonic. "Got ambitions to go into counseling, have you, sweetheart? Tell me, how is your own relationship going? Obviously, Tom hasn't got a firm grip on what you need if you're sneaking out and disobeying him. Is he meeting all your needs or is he ignoring them in favor of his own?"

Frankie gaped at him, surprised at the attack.

"Roarke," Sam said in a shocked voice.

Roarke just stared at her through half-lidded eyes. Obviously, he expected her to run crying from the room. But Frankie was made of tougher stuff than that. She'd grown up with four older brothers.

She firmed her shoulders. "You're trying to make me angry so I back off. Does that work well with other people? I bet you've pushed away everyone but Sam. How's that working out for you? Are you happy?"

Roarke narrowed his gaze at her.

"You know what? Maybe Tom's not the problem here. Maybe it's you. You're so busy blaming yourself that you've pushed away everyone who needed you, who loves you. Did you ever think about your family's pain? Obviously, they didn't just lose one son, but two."

Frankie cursed herself as soon as she said it. Who was she to tell this man how to run his life? She didn't even have control over her own most of the time.

"I'm not the only one who blames me, Frankie. Your husband hates my guts for what I did."

The door to the office creaked. She glanced around in shock.

"I don't hate you," Tom said quietly as he walked into the office. "And it's not just you I blame." His gaze hit Frankie, running over her body as though to make sure she was all right.

"Brax called you, huh?" she asked weakly.

He nodded. "I was on my way home. My last appointment cancelled." Tonight was his late night at the clinic.

"I'm sorry for disobeying you," she said quickly, hoping her immediate apology would ease the anger in his eyes.

"We'll get to that later," he promised ominously. He held out his hand to her. "Let's go."

Frankie rose, feeling defeat pound at her. She hadn't fixed anything. In fact, she'd possibly made things worse. Plus, she was going to get her ass spanked, and all for nothing.

"Thank you," Sam whispered as he stood and gave her a hug. "I've been trying to get him to talk about this for years."

"I think I made things worse," she whispered back.

"Chin up, sweetheart." He let her go and gave her a gentle smile. He morphed from gorgeous to breathtakingly stunning. She shook her head to clear it before walking over to take Tom's hand. Tom turned to leave.

"Tom," Roarke called out. "Wait. Please."

Tom stilled but didn't look back.

"I'm sorry. I'm sorry I'm the reason he died," Roarke told him, his voice thick with emotion. "I'm sorry I had to make the decision to stop his life support."

Tom stared at the far wall. "I loved him and I blamed you for taking him from me. He was my family." Frankie squeezed his hand. She knew Tom's parents had never been there for him.

"You were always part of our family, from the day Austin brought you home."

Tom took a deep breath and turned then tugged her against his side. "I've been doing a lot of thinking over the past few weeks, about why I'm so angry with you. Why I hate you. And I realized it was because blaming you was easier than dealing with my own guilt. You gave me a convenient target to aim my anger at, instead of focusing it on myself, where it really belonged."

Tom paused and Frankie patted his arm, trying to lend him her strength. "I'd already argued with Austin before you got there. I told him that the clubs weren't for me, that I wanted something more. I didn't want to play. I enjoyed the discipline aspect, but not the rest. He was furious with me. I was surprised by his reaction, I hadn't really expected it. Most of the time, I just watched. I only went there because he asked me too. Then you came along to talk to him about Cara and it pushed him over the edge. When you made the decision to turn off his life support, I was filled with fury. I didn't deal with any of it well. Over the years my anger has faded, but my guilt has grown. When I learned you'd spoken to Frankie, I over-reacted. Badly. I'm sorry, Roarke."

Frankie stared at Sam with wide eyes, seeing the shock on his own face. This night had taken a turn she hadn't expected. She'd thought it would take months of work to get both men to the point they were at right now.

"He thought he would lose you. That's why he was so angry," Roarke said quietly. "You weren't to blame for his death, Tom. I guess neither of us were. The guy who hit him was."

It was a break through, she thought. Even though the tension was still there at least they'd admitted that Austin's death, while tragic and unnecessary, was not their fault.

Tom nodded and Frankie felt him relax his tense muscles. "If you'll excuse us, I have to get my wife home, then she and I are going to have a long talk about following orders."

Damn. Frankie gulped.

"Would you like to come over for dinner?" Frankie blurted out, surprising herself. Everyone looked at her. She flushed. "Maybe next Sunday night, around seven? Both of you, of course." She looked around Tom to Sam, who smiled.

Roarke looked at Tom. Frankie held her breath.

"Yes, please do," Tom said stiffly.

Roarke nodded. "We'd like that."

"And by that time, Frankie might actually be able to sit comfortably."

Frankie gulped. Oh shit.

12

"**U**pstairs," Tom ordered as soon as they walked into their house. "Strip and lie naked on your back on the bed. I want you to hold your legs up against your chest."

"Tom," she protested.

"Now," he barked.

Unused to hearing that level of anger in his voice, she fled, racing upstairs. Oh God, what had she done? Sure, she'd had only the best intentions, but she'd disobeyed Tom and now he was furious with her.

Stripping, Frankie lay on her back as ordered then pulled her legs up to her chest, clasping her hands under her knees to hold them there. This position was so humiliating.

Tom walked into the room, rolling back the arms of his shirt. "Leg's wider apart."

"Tom, shouldn't we talk about this?" she asked as she saw the plastic bag in his hand. The bag that was kept in the fridge with a carved piece of ginger in it. Fuck.

"I think you've talked enough for one night, don't you, Frankie?" He moved to the wardrobe and pulled out the box that held his instruments of torture. Oh shit, what was she in for, tonight?

"But I only had the best intentions, and it worked, didn't it? You and Roarke are talking." No matter what punishment he gave her, it was worth it to have the two of them speaking again.

"I know you had good intentions, Frankie," Tom said calmly. He stood and walked over to her, placing a pair of gloves and the bag down on the side table. "But you disobeyed me and once again put yourself in danger. You had no business going to a BDSM club by yourself. You have no idea of the protocols. What if you'd found yourself in a situation you couldn't get out of? Not to mention you lied to me, and yet again, impulsively ran off without letting me know where you were."

"I left a note," she told him quickly. "In case you got back first. It's by the phone."

He stared down at her and nodded. "That's good. It doesn't excuse your actions, though. Anything could have happened to you there without me to protect you. Not to mention, I told you not to speak to Roarke again, and yet you deliberately sought him out."

"You were being pigheaded. And besides, it all worked out. The two of you needed to speak to each other properly. I'd say overall it was quite a successful night, wouldn't you?"

He smacked his hand down on her bare butt. Frankie gasped.

"It was my business, Frankie. You had no right to interfere."

"I was never in any danger, Tom. I chose tonight because it was newbie night. I did some research before I went along. Of course, I didn't expect Brax to be there."

Tom raised his brows. "And that's someone else you owe an apology to, Frankie. You gave Brax the shock of his life, and then when he tried to remove you from a situation you had no business being in, you sassed him and gave him trouble."

"I still think I did the right thing."

"Who is in charge here?" he asked her in a deep voice.

"You are."

"Do you want to change that?"

What? "No. You know I don't."

"Did you put yourself in a situation that you knew I wouldn't approve of, that could have ended in disaster?"

Well, shit. "Yes."

"And did you disobey me?"

She nearly squirmed. "Yes."

"And what does that mean?"

"That you're going to punish me."

"Yes, I am." He reached for the gloves, pulling them on before opening the small plastic bag and pulling out the ginger. It had already been skinned and carved into a small plug.

Frankie's gaze was riveted on the piece of ginger. He'd threatened it a few times but she had yet to experience it.

"Reach down and pull your ass cheeks apart."

"No lube?" she squeaked. He always used lube when he plugged her.

"This is much smaller than your plug. And lube prevents the oil from doing its job."

"And I guess we wouldn't want that."

He raised his eyebrows. "We wouldn't. Hold your cheeks apart, if I have to ask again, I'll punish your bottom hole."

Holy shit. He wouldn't. Although from the look on his face it seemed like it was definitely an option. She quickly pulled her cheeks apart.

"It's not very long or big," he told her as she whimpered.

He was right, it was far smaller than her plug and it felt cool.

But just the thought of it in her ass made her uncomfortable. She wished she could expel it.

"Keep it there, Frankie. If it comes out, then I'll get a bigger one," Tom warned.

Immediately she clenched down and her ass started to warm as the oil escaped the root. It wasn't that bad, though, and she relaxed a little. Okay, maybe this wouldn't be so bad.

Tom used one arm to press her legs back even further to her chest. "Let's start your spanking. Why are you being spanked?"

"For disobeying you, interfering in stuff that wasn't my business and putting myself in a potentially bad situation. Although I'd like to protest that last one."

"Protest noted." With his other hand, he started spanking her. Each time his hand landed she clenched her buttocks against the sting. It wasn't long until the ginger oil went from warm to burning her insides.

Shit. Shit. Shit. This sucked.

Frankie screwed her eyes up tight. She wasn't sure what stung more the heat inside, or the one Tom was creating on the outside. Tears tracked down her cheeks as she started to sob. She wiggled back and forth, wanting to get free. She couldn't take any more. His hand never faltered as he smacked it down on her bottom until it was throbbing.

"Please, no more," she begged. "Tom. Please."

"Oh honey," he said with sympathy. "It's far too early in the night for you to be begging." He landed a few more smacks on her ass. "Roll over. I want you on your hands and knees, legs wide."

With a sob, she carefully rolled over, not wanting to lose the ginger inside her.

TOM LOOKED DOWN at his wife. When he'd gotten the call from Brax telling him that she was at Indulgence, he'd been instantly filled with fear. She had no business at a BDSM club, certainly not without him.

He shuddered to think what might have happened to her. Any Dom worth his salt would have snapped her up in an instant. She was gorgeous, fiery, and with a definite submissive streak. Someone else might try to break her spirit. Not Tom, he liked her fire, her sassiness. As long as she didn't put her safety in jeopardy or outright disrespect or disobey him.

"Lean down, rest your chest on the bed. This isn't going to be over quickly, I want you comfortable."

She snorted. "I hardly think I'm going to be all that comfortable.

He smiled a little in acknowledgment. "Your butt certainly won't be. You disobeyed me, Frankie. You didn't honor the fact that I asked you to stay out of this."

"Asked?" she protested. "You didn't ask, you ordered me."

"Hush, little girl. Now is the time for you to be quiet and try to soothe me, not rile me up more."

She settled down and he continued. "I do not take your safety lightly. This is going to be hard, Frankie, because I can't have you continuously risking yourself. Do you understand? I do this because I love you."

"I understand."

"Good. I want you to stay very still. I'm going to take the ginger out. Then you are getting twenty strokes of my belt and I'll finish with five of the cane."

FRANKIE GASPED. "PLEASE, TOM, NO," she begged. She hated the cane, had only experienced it once before and she'd sworn to herself that she'd never risk having him use it on her again.

"I'm sorry, sweetheart, I don't like punishing you so hard, but this has to stop. You have to start taking greater care with your safety. Now, remember, I expect you to stay still otherwise I'll have to tie you down."

He quickly removed the ginger from her bottom. At least that was one less thing to worry about.

"All right, we're starting with the belt."

Frankie cried out as the belt slapped down on her already stinging buttocks. Tom swung it steadily, without respite. The sound it made was almost worse than the sting, although that was no fun either. Especially on a freshly spanked butt. He didn't falter, didn't stop, no matter how much she cried and begged for him to.

By the time he'd counted out twenty, she was sobbing, her buttocks on fire as she swayed back and forth, trying to find some relief, somehow.

"Please, Tom, I can't take it. Please," she begged

"You're doing so well, baby. That's twenty now. Good girl," Tom soothed her, running his hand over her back as she cried.

"I'm sorry, I'm sorry," she repeated over and over.

"I know, baby. Almost over. These last five with the cane are for putting yourself in danger. I know you don't think you were, but you're such an innocent, sweetheart. You have no idea of your appeal. You must pay more attention to your own safety. I want you to count these out for me, then thank me and ask for another."

Crying, she screamed as the cane slashed down, leaving a burning strip on her already swollen, hot buttocks.

"O-one, Sir. Thank you. M-may I have another?"

By the time five came around, she could barely get the words out through her tears. The bedspread was completely soaked beneath her face. She was a mess. In so much pain she wasn't even sure she could move.

Tom lay on the bed, gathering her close so she lay on her side, her face tucked into his firm chest. As she cried, he rocked her gently, crooning to her softly, rubbing her back.

"I'm sorry, I'm sorry," she said hoarsely, her voice nearly gone.

"Shh, baby. All is forgiven. Just let me hold you. Let me hold you close and know that I love you more than words."

"Ditto," she replied.

EPILOGUE

O ne week later...

FRANKIE FRANTICALLY MOVED around the kitchen, cooking up a storm. Sam and Roarke were coming for dinner tonight and she wanted things to be perfect.

"Frankie, calm down," Tom said quietly as she ran over to the oven.

She'd forgotten about the bread!

"Damn," she swore as she pulled out the clearly burned loaves. "They're ruined."

"Language," Tom cautioned her, glowering. But she had no time to pay attention to the warning. Instead of reaching for an oven mitt, she used the towel to pick up the tray. The thin towel gave little protection against the hot tray and she yelped as she burned her hand.

"Shit, shit, shit," she cried, tears filling her eyes. Nothing was working out. This was going to be a disaster.

"Here, let me see," Tom said calmly as he moved up beside her. He pulled her over to the sink and turned on the cold water and stuck her hand underneath it. "Leave it there," he said warningly as she tried to move away to close the oven door.

"I don't have time. I have to make more bread."

"I will go to the store and buy some bread."

"Bought bread!" she squealed. "You can't serve them bought bread."

"Why not?" he said incredulously. "It's what we eat every day. Frankie, I want you to calm down right now. You've sworn twice in the last couple of minutes. I'm being lenient with you right now. But you're working yourself up into a state and if you don't settle yourself down, I'm going to have to do it for you."

"I don't have time to calm down. I'm cooking dinner. And it's a damn mess," she wailed.

Smack! Smack!

Tom gave her a short, sharp spanking over her pants as she stood with her hand under the cold water.

He stopped suddenly and leaning in close, kissed her neck tenderly.

"It's not a mess. You're acting crazy, woman. It's just dinner."

"It's not just dinner. It needs to be perfect." She was near tears, her emotions shot to hell.

Tom wrapped his arms around her from behind. "You're trying too hard, sweetheart. You need to let things just happen as they happen, okay?"

Frankie took a deep breath. He was right. She was acting like a maniac.

"Now, I want you to take a deep breath and calm down. I'm going to go get some burn cream for your hand then wrap it up. Then I will help you with dinner, all right?"

"Yes, Sir," she replied.

"That's my good girl." He patted her bottom as he left. "And keep that hand where it is."

The last couple of months had been a real roller coaster for her. Her obsession with getting pregnant, their trip to the cabin, her visit to see Roarke. Yes, life had certainly had its ups and downs lately. But she felt she'd needed to go through everything to get to where she was now. Tom had always been the leader in their relationship, but lately he'd taken an even stronger role, particularly in the bedroom and she loved it.

They were both happier, and his relationship with Roarke, while still stiff and uncertain, was coming along.

Her love. Her man. Her old-fashioned husband.

All in all, Frankie figured that while her butt might not have approved of her actions, things had ended up pretty good.

Not perfect.

But she was fine with that. Because she wouldn't change a thing.

EXCERPT FROM HIS OLD-FASHIONED LOVE

Brax leaned forward and grabbed hold of her hand. Heat instantly sizzled its way up her arm, spreading throughout her body. She pressed her legs together as her clit throbbed in reaction.

Wow.

"Sweetheart, I love that you want to help me, but you are not going with me. This is between me and Mason—"

"And his brothers if they're around. You can't go up against three of them by yourself."

"Don't worry. I can take care of myself. And you."

"I don't need you to take care of me," she said, surprised.

"That so? You seem like you could do with someone watching out for you. You need a keeper, young lady. Some of your choices haven't been very wise decisions."

"Like what?" She always thought of herself as quite sensible. Steady. Boring.

"Let's see... getting involved in the middle of a fight with men much bigger than you. Going for a walk at night when your leg was paining you, without telling anyone where you were. Walking around a vandalized, empty building site instead of staying in your car and calling the sheriff. And right now, you're insisting on coming with me to meet a guy who likes to hit women. Do you ever think before you rush into things?"

"Of course I do, usually. When you put it like that it doesn't sound that great. But I had good reasons for doing each of those things."

"I'm sure you thought so at the time, but in each case you compromised your safety and that makes me worry about you. I don't want anything bad touching you and that definitely includes Mason Philips. You'll stay here where I don't have to worry about you getting hurt."

"I can protect your back, Brax. I'm not completely helpless."

He smiled at her. "You're not helpless at all. But like I said before, I'm an old-fashioned guy, sweetheart. It's my privilege to take care of those smaller and more fragile than me. That includes you. So while you are capable of taking on the world, I am always going to stand between you and danger."

Holy hell. She couldn't get any words out. He was the type of man she had always dreamed of.

Made in the USA
Columbia, SC
30 August 2023

22308743R00090